Centre o

An imagined h
of Rennes-le-Château

Cathar and Château Quéribus

Centre of the Universe

An imagined history of the mystery of Rennes-le-Château

Bryan Andrews

First published 2019
Copyright © Bryan Andrews

Bryan Andrews asserts the moral right to be identified as the author
of this work

ISBN: 978 0 953 80429 0

ILLUSTRATIONS
Paintings are by Bryan Andrews
Photographs are by Bryan Andrews
Stock photographs of Emma Calvé, Gare Perpignan
and Bérenger Saunière

BIBLIOGRAPHY

The Holy Blood and the Holy Grail
- Michael Baigent, Richard Leigh and Henry Lincoln
The Woman with the Alabaster Jar - Margaret Starbird
The Perfect Heresy - Stephen O'Shea
The Portal - Patrice Chaplin
The DaVinci Code - Dan Brown
Labyrinth - Kate Mosse
The Expected One - Kathleen McGowan
Montaillou - Emmanuel Le Roy Ladurie

A catalogue record for this book is available from the British Library.

Set in Goudy Old Style by Ken Boyter
Cover, book design and typeset by Ken Boyter www.kenboyter.co.uk

THANKS

My thanks to Ken Boyter for the typesetting and cover design; to Kate Miller, leader of the Hertford Writers Circle, for her encouragement and proof reading; to my partner Ruth Rankin for her encouragement of my writing; to my sons Clive and Mike Andrews for their advice and encouragement and to the Hertford Writers' Circle for their ongoing and helpful support. Also the opportunity provided by my Languedoc House and the friends who shared its purchase Dina Glouberman, Clare Manifold, Sue Richards, Julie McNamara and Jerry Doyle.

DEDICATION

Dedicated to my wonderful partner Ruth, and my fantastic sons, Clive and Mike, with heartfelt thanks for their support at all times.

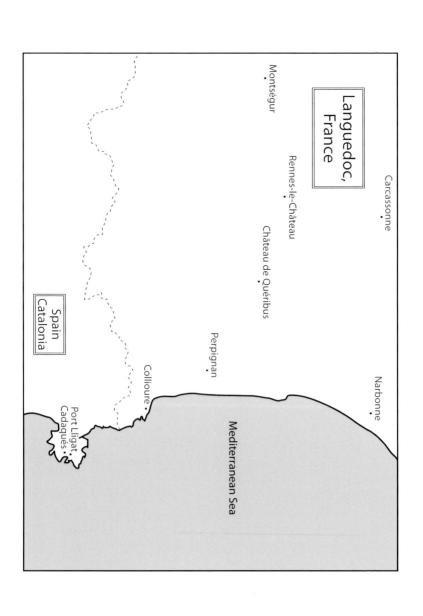

Languedoc,
France

Spain
Catalonia

Montségur

Carcassonne

Rennes-le-Château

Château de Quéribus

Perpignan

Narbonne

Collioure

Port Lligat
Cadaqués

Mediterranean Sea

Chapter 1

Languedoc 2004

Going off on a holiday on his own was not something Bernard had been used to. There were the years of taking his young family on camping holidays in France and Italy, but after the divorce he hadn't bothered much with holidays, simply because he had no one to go with. But now the idea was surfacing. Languedoc, time for himself, investigating the story of the Cathars and going to that little village called Rennes-le-Château, all this sounded suddenly so appealing he felt enthusiastic about taking a holiday. So, now, there he was, going through security at Stansted airport.

Bernard was fascinated by the Cathars. Though these enigmatic 'heretics' were massacred by the Catholic Inquisition in the thirteenth century, they seemed to Bernard to be much closer to his own time than the Victorians. Some said they were the first Protestants, predating Luther by a couple of hundred years. He thought of their strange similarity with the Quakers, who centuries later had promoted the idea that there was no need for a priest to mediate, as Christ lived within everyone. He admired the Cathars' peaceful and simple way of life and their acceptance of living together without marriage. All this seemed mysteriously close to ideas which had resurfaced in recent times.

On the other hand, he was very unsure of their basic philosophy of dualism, which said that everything on earth was the creation of the devil and everything of the spirit came from God. It seemed intolerably sad to reject all the delights of being human and to believe, as they did, that their bodies were a kind of 'tunic' which they were forced to inhabit and would be mercifully released from on death.

On his first day in the Languedoc he made the excursion – or pilgrimage – to the Château de Quéribus, where the Cathars had withstood a siege; the awesome castle perched high in the sky where eagles flew. The climb was steep and the ticket seller warned about the wind: "Tenez bien votre chapeau monsieur." Quéribus appeared to have been carved out of the rock by some giant hand. No other tourists were around, the clouds were low and Bernard felt he was entering a place packed with mysteries and legend. His heart quickened as, finally, he was standing in the ancient chapel, its magnificent column still soaring up to the vaulted roof like prayers ascending to heaven. The stories of the mediaeval Cathar Parfaits were held in the very stones. They were called Parfaits in mockery by the Catholic church – the perfect ones.

"Bonjour." The voice took him by surprise, as he hadn't noticed the young woman standing in the shadows. She had a digital camera in her hand and was dressed in a blue and strangely unfashionable coat.

"Oh bonjour. I didn't see you there... Excusez moi je ne

Château Quéribus

Guilhem l'Hérétique Vin Rouge

parle français bien," he blurted in his stumbling French.

"Pas de problème, I speak English," she replied.

She had noticed Bernard trying to read a notice on the wall in the Salle du Pilier. "It's in Occitan," she explained. "That's the ancient language of this region. In mediaeval times everyone spoke Occitan but now there is only one village near here where it is still spoken. Languedoc means the langue d'Oc, the language of 'yes' – oc meant yes in this part of France."

Bernard thanked her and carried on his tour of the fantastic château, which seemed to him like the throne of a mountain god. Later he spotted the woman again in the village at the foot of the mountain. He had wanted to visit the little church in Cucugnan to see its golden statues and there she was. He watched as she lit a candle and placed it by the statue of La Vierge Enceinte, the pregnant Virgin. The flame leapt up and flickered with an intensity that was brighter than the other candles. She passed near him as she left the church; he was aware of her perfume. It was enchanting and unlike anything he had smelt before.

Bernard wandered along the village street. It bordered a green valley below undulating hills, which swept dizzily up to the château perched on its scrag of rock. The mysteries of the area were one thing but the lure of a good French lunch was another. The Michelin had guided him to the Auberge du Vigneron and soon he was nestling a glass of Kir in his hand and anticipating a tasty confit de canard. The confit was superb but the tarte aux framboises, which followed, was ecstasy.

As he took the last delicious mouthful, he noticed her sitting alone on the terrace. She, too, was at the dessert stage. The wine had relaxed him enough to take a risk. A little shyly, he walked over to her table and asked: "May I join you for coffee?" She smiled her assent and soon they were past the introductions and first pleasantries.

Her name was Madeleine, she lived in Paris near the Gare St Lazare and was an executive in an advertising agency in the Champs Elysées. They talked earnestly about what had drawn them to Quéribus: the Cathars, the Knights Templars and Mary Magdalene. He was excited to discover she shared his enthusiasm for the mysteries; in fact she seemed to know more than he did. "Have you ever read Arthur Guirdham?" she asked. Bernard had vaguely heard of him as having written something about people who thought they were reincarnated Cathars. "If you are going to talk about reincarnation, I need another drink. How about a bottle of Fitou, since it's from this region?" he suggested.

Madeleine agreed. "This one sounds interesting, it's called Guilhem L'Hérétique," she said. "It must be named after the last Cathar, Guilhem Bélibaste, who was burned at a village near here." Bernard was thrilled at this encounter with a wine which connected him immediately to the Cathar story.

After the first glass, she began to talk more animatedly. Apparently Arthur Guirdham was an English psychiatrist who had discovered that several of his patients had independently shown signs of being reincarnated Cathar

Perfects. One woman had even recalled dreams in the ancient Oc language. Madeleine believed herself to be a reincarnation of Esclarmonde of Foix, a Cathar woman Perfect. Esclarmonde was a preacher of great persuasiveness and beauty. She had upset the Catholic Abbot of Toulouse when she countered his theological arguments with authority.

"She offended him simply by being a woman saying such things!" Madeleine told him. "I have a clear memory of being at Montségur when we were under siege and the terrible moment when we all agreed to walk down the mountain and throw ourselves into the flames of the pyres which the soldiers had built. I can even see the blue dress I was wearing. Approaching the flames, choking on the smoke, God, that was a horrible moment."

She paused, took a sip of wine and Bernard could see the fear in her eyes as if it were happening now. Should he believe her or was she a bit crazy? The force of her feelings persuaded him to listen without scoffing at her story. Yet if her story was true he was witnessing a memory of something that had happened more than 750 years ago!

She stopped talking, a little breathless with emotion, flicked back her long dark hair and then asked if he would like to go with her tomorrow to the Château de Montségur. She wanted to go back there to come to terms with the experience of remembering something so awful that it was affecting her life now.

"I would like your company if you have nothing else

planned," she said. Bernard was transfixed. Here was this lovely French woman, asking him to go with her to one of the places he had dreamed of seeing for years.

"There is nothing I would like more," he smiled.

Montségur came into view as they rounded the corner of a narrow road. The old castle straddled a huge rounded mound of earth, impossibly high, with ramparts so sheer it looked as if the only way up was with grappling irons. But an hour later Bernard and Madeleine found themselves walking through the arched gateway into the castle keep. The walk up had been tough but far from impossible.

Sitting on the old rocks inside the castle walls, Madeleine and Bernard felt the strangeness of this place, built so long ago but carrying such powerful memories of the ten month siege and suffering of the Cathar men and women that it still pulled to its summit all kinds of seekers. Not only hikers but Cathar devotees, New Agers, lovers of esoteric mysteries and holidaymakers who had seen it in their guide books.

Madeleine was elated; the clear air up here after the heat of the walk was something of a surprise. She drank deeply from a Volvic bottle and sighed as she gazed at the castle's ruined walls. She tried to clothe its skeleton, to form a whole picture of a living community in its walls. Now she wanted to close her eyes and meditate on being here at last. Could she re-live the past and free herself from it?

There was nothing particularly magic or mysterious in the way that Esclarmonde appeared. There she was standing in front of Madeleine. It was the last day, 16 March 1244, when

Cathar Memorial, Montségur

they had been ordered to convert to Catholicism or burn. After a noisy meeting in the Great Hall they had all voted for death. What a strange thing to vote for. Even some of the soldiers and non-Cathars, who had been caught up with the others when the entire Cathar population went to Montségur, decided to become Cathars and die with them.

Esclarmonde had been used to exerting power. Now she was surrendering it to the enemy but she had no misgivings about her decision, she told Madeleine.

"After all, it would be impossible to choose life and to not live by my own truth, my belief in dualism, in the equality of women with men and everything beautiful that is Catharism." But Madeleine saw Esclarmonde's fear too. "Oh, trapped in these bodies which we call tunics, we fear just as much as a Catholic when we are going to burn. To feel the flames, to inhale and choke on the smoke, to hear the screams of our friends... this is terrible and we know what Jesus meant when he said in the Garden of Gethsemane, Father take this cup away from me!"

Madeleine herself was breathing hard as she listened to Esclarmonde's account of that terrible day. Esclarmonde told how the fear had almost weakened her resolve but she had done what she could for Catharism's survival. The night before, it had been agreed that three Cathars would climb down the vertiginous north face of Montségur, taking the Cathar treasure and sacred documents with them. The three were chosen for their climbing ability, but otherwise were ordinary Cathars. If they survived the dangerous climb they would probably not be caught on that side of the mountain and so the treasure could be taken to safety. Esclarmonde herself had been chosen as the one to hand the treasured document to Pierre, Hugo and Authie. The Cathar treasure and the secret parchment were carefully wrapped and put in a leather bag. At the moment of handing the bag to Pierre, Esclarmonde had recited some words from the consolamentum ritual to release the treasure to its new hiding place over the mountains.

Madeleine opened her eyes. She was back. The experience had been so intense, but was it real? Was it a visualisation or was Esclarmonde appearing to her? She was enough of a modern Parisian to be a sceptic. She had been brought up to admire Descartes and the high value the French put on rationality.

Bernard had been exploring Montségur and was eager to talk to Madeleine about his impressions.

"This is such an important place in Western history because it marks the first genocide," he said. "Yet it's so beautiful. It's as if Auschwitz had been set in paradise. Did you know the Nazis were interested in this place? There is even a record of Goebbels flying over Montségur on the 700th anniversary of the massacre in 1944. Could a creed which embraced genocide admire a sect which preached love? No, I'm convinced their obsession was more to do with the Nazis' psychic connection with the Inquisition and the persecutors of Catharism."

On their way down, they stopped at the monument at the

foot of the hill: a stone Cathar cross where people still left flowers to mark the deaths of more than 50 Perfects and 150 ordinary Cathars whose lives had ended in the flames.

Madeleine confided to Bernard her experience of encountering Esclarmonde at the top of Montségur. Bernard didn't comment, but he listened without dismissing her story. He felt even more certain that this woman was either mad or psychic, but he tended to the latter as she was too straightforward and intelligent, when not reporting esoteric visions, to be crazy.

"Perhaps the strangest thing about Montségur is that it is nowhere near a place of strategic importance," Madeleine was saying. "So people have speculated about why it was built. Some believe it was a temple. There is a pentagon shape in the form of the walls, which esoterically links the earth with the zodiac. It could even be the tabernacle of the Holy Grail – maybe this is why it was so important to the Cathars..."

Bernard decided a sensible response was called for. "Come on. Let's find a café and get a drink," he said, as he held her arm to negotiate a tricky bit of the final descent, and she laughingly agreed.

Rennes-le-Château Church Door
"Terribilis est locus iste"

Chapter 2

Rennes-le-Château

Their next stop was the little hilltop village of Rennes-le-Château some 40 km away over the mountain which separated Montségur country from the Corbières.

"What have you brought me here for?" demanded Madeleine as she slammed the door of her hired silver Peugeot and surveyed the valley below where Visigoths had built their now vanished city of Razès.

"Have you ever heard of Bérenger Saunière?"

"Non, jamais," she replied.

"He was the parish priest here in the late 19th century and he may have discovered your Cathar treasure hidden in or near his church."

"Oh yes," she replied doubtfully, "and I suppose he gave it to the Vatican so they could keep it out of sight for all these years."

"It's even stranger than that," said Bernard. "He became fabulously rich after discovering something and spent huge amounts which no parish priest could possibly have on rebuilding his church and building that fantastic tower over there which he called Tour Magdala."

"Maybe he'd been selling indulgences. They used to you know," said Madeleine.

"Now it's your turn to be the cynic."

Then Bernard told her the dream he had years ago. A dream which had so affected him that it had led him to new discoveries. The dream took place in a restaurant where a young waitress was being unnecessarily rude to the dreamer and instead of taking his order she whacked him on the shoulder with a rolled up newspaper. The other diners looked round horrified and said she should be punished. The crowd of diners led him to an underground cavern and he began to dig a grave there. In the dream it seemed just that she should be buried there and he began to dig with the crowd silently supporting him. He looked round and saw as vividly as anything he had ever seen in a dream, Jesus standing there with a look of deep anger and disapproval at what he was doing.

A member of the crowd said, "Do you know what you're doing? You're burying his girlfriend!" And he knew this was not a waitress, it was Mary Magdalene!

"Zut, quel rêve!" Madeleine exclaimed.

"Exactly, that's what I thought at the time and it was news to me that Christ could ever have had a girlfriend. It felt like a revelation which had been made to me but basically it seemed then to be a bit blasphemous too. It was some years later that I heard the story from another source when Scorsese's film 'The Last Temptation of Christ' came out and there were protests in Leicester Square by people who didn't like the idea of Jesus being portrayed in a sexual relationship. And now the idea is so current I am amazed that I had that dream.

When you think about it, it was unheard of for a man not to be married in that culture.

"Later I came here to Rennes-le-Château. I was staying at a friend's farm nearby and by chance discovered this place and, for me, the whole thing took off, the mystery of the treasure, the Mary Magdalene obsession of Saunière, the building of the Tour Magdala. All the pieces began to fit into place and I realised that the dream which had come to me was actually the same information that had inspired researchers like Henry Lincoln to write 'The Holy Blood and the Holy Grail'".

Madeleine said, "Look, I really want to go to the hotel now as I've got to catch up with finishing a report I am writing and have to send off to Paris tonight. After that I'll get an early night. Perhaps meet you at breakfast," she smiled.

"OK. I think I'll hang around and explore for a bit and walk down the hill."

It was the strangest message to find inscribed above the church entrance: "Terribilis est locus iste." (This place is terrible). The door gave to Bernard's touch and creaked open. A wave of myrrh incense hung in the air. The first shock was the statue, which stood menacingly in front of him as he entered. Bernard had never seen anything so hideous. Not even Hieronymus Bosch could have come up with this stooped creature with its diabolical smile. What was it doing here in this church in a small French village?

The rest of the church was crudely beautiful if you like glossily painted alabaster saints and golden angels. Bernard felt so affected by the atmosphere that he had to sit on an uncomfortable wooden chair and ponder the strangeness of this place. He was fascinated by the odd paintings of the Stations of the Cross, which seemed unlike those he had seen in other Catholic churches. When he finally got up to go it was dusk and the light in the church was getting dim. He was hungry now and fancied a good French dinner and a glass of wine. Turning the door handle he found it stiff and resistant. The huge wooden door was locked. He looked around for some help, maybe something he could use as a tool and jumped back on his heels as he met the mocking gaze of the ghastly statue of Asmodeus, the incarnation of the devil, lit by a beam of light coming from an upper window. Frustrated by his useless attempts to force the large wooden door, he began to resign himself to spending some time here. The most likely explanation for his predicament was that the verger, or whoever he was, had not seen him sitting quietly in the shadows and locked the church for the night.

"My mobile phone!" he exclaimed with relief as he pulled it from his rucksack. The little light came on and then flickered and went out.

"Damn," he had forgotten to recharge the battery. He sighed with despair at his entrapment, tried a few bangs on the door and then decided that if he was going to spend the night here it was definitely not going to be close to the devilish statue, which guarded the door.

Scrabbling around for somewhere to make himself

comfortable he tripped and fell. Slightly bruised he noticed his fall had dislodged a paving stone. Struggling to replace it he noticed something trapped between the stone and the earth underneath. Curious, he pulled it out and found himself holding a small packet. By the light of the moon bathing him in light from an overhead window he opened it and found the surprising contents. A letter written in Spanish and a yellow cardboard ticket. Feeling uneasy he glanced at Asmodeus. To his horror the beast turned its head slowly, its eyes burning red, and then slowly turned its head back.

"My imagination is getting the better of me... that couldn't have happened," he reasoned.

The next morning the verger was surprised to discover a man asleep curled up on a pew, a backpack for a pillow.

Bernard met Madeleine at the five star Hôtel des Ducs de Joyeuse for an elegant breakfast in the converted mediaeval château.

"You'll never guess how I spent the night," said Bernard over croissants and a big cup of café crème. After recounting his uncomfortable night he said, "I'd like to show you Saunière's church."

She was a bit puzzled at Bernard's excitement when later that morning he led her hurriedly in the direction of a quite ordinary looking village church. Well, until she had got up close and he pointed out the inscription above the door. And then she was startled to see as they entered a hideous looking creature guarding the door. "Asmodeus the devil," said

Bernard, "also known as a guardian of treasure."

"Quelle surprise! What is he doing in here?"

"There's more," said Bernard, pointing out the starry ceiling above the altar and there, kneeling with her alabaster jar the focal point of the whole thing, Mary Magdalene. "Bérenger developed this obsession with Mary Magdalene, dedicated his church to her, built her the tower I showed you yesterday. You could say he was a devoted disciple of hers, venerated her, but maybe he had discovered something really special about her. Being in here all night it was terrible and wonderful. I saw amazing things just like Howard Carter."

"Qui est lui?"

"You know, the guy who discovered Tutankhamun's treasure."

"You found treasure?"

"Not exactly, but...look Madeleine," he urged "will you come with me to Perpignan, now?"

"Calmez vous," soothed Madeleine.

"No, listen to me. I have discovered something amazing and if you want to come with me, trust me... it's the next step I need to take."

"Mais non, I do not want to rush off. I want to see a little more of this village and I want you to tell me what happened in the church before we go anywhere."

They walked though the village, exploring the gardens of the Villa Bethania where Saunière had lived and entertained his wealthy guests like Emma Calvé, the internationally famous opera singer from Paris. At the Tour Magdala they looked out over the fantastic landscape of the valley where the ancient Visigoth town of Razès once dominated the region.

"I was pretty scared in the church when I realised I couldn't get out. When I was looking around in the semi darkness I tripped over a loose flagstone. I tried to put it back in place and a piece crumbled away and under it I found the strangest thing. What I saw convinced me I need to go to Perpignan to check up on it. Will you come with me now?"

"Ah bien, I have finished my report so I am free... for une petite aventure."

Mary Magdalene, Saunière Altar painting

Chapter 3

Perpignan, the Centre of the Universe

They checked their things out of the hotel and Bernard felt his luck was in as he set off with this strange woman on an adventure together. Making for Perpignan on the D616 Madeleine took a wrong turning and they found themselves in the village of Axat. She asked a passer-by for directions to Perpignan.

"Un train part en dix minutes. C'est plus vite que la voiture."

"Let's park the car and get it," Madeleine said "we could be there in time for lunch. You know in France you have to be in a restaurant by 1.30 or they will not serve you."

"That's one thing I don't like about France," commented Bernard.

The train was a tourist train with an open deck.

"This is a crazy little train and we're getting wet," complained Madeleine as the rain fell and tourists began to huddle to avoid it as best they could.

"Not such a good idea after all," said Bernard, "but at least we're getting there."

And then came an announcement of a fault on the line which meant the train would be stopping at the next station until it was fixed.

A smartly dressed, good looking woman in her forties sitting in the next seat, addressed them, "Hi, I overheard you guys talking about Perpignan. I've got a car parked at St Paul so I could take you there if you like."

The train pulled in to the little station of St Paul de Fenouillet. Relieved, Madeleine and Bernard sat in the back of the black BMW as Diane proved to be an expert at beating the French at their own game of overtaking on dangerous bends.

"But this isn't the way to Perpignan. Look," whispered Madeleine to Bernard as the car lurched past a Perpignan sign pointing in the other direction. The car began to zoom up a steep hill with a precarious drop on the side.

"Where are you going?" demanded Bernard.

Gare de Perpignan

"Relax honey, this is the scenic route," Diane cracked back.

They came to a stop at the summit of one of the highest points around, Força Réal. A telecommunications aerial pierced the bright blue sky.

"Hey guys I'd better explain…I'm a guide, well I volunteer sometimes, at the Rennes-le-Château museum so of course I'm really interested in this old mystery and I overheard you say you'd found something in the church. Well I'm in there regularly and I've never found anything new so I hope you'll excuse me for kinda hijacking you. I want to find out what it was and show you something in return. That's why I drove you up here - I wanted to show you this before you go to Perpignan."

They stood at the edge of the viewing platform with its orientation map. Diane swept her arm around to the left.

"Over there that's Perpignan, to the South, Spain, that's where Hannibal crossed the Pyrénées. People always associate Hannibal with crossing the Alps but he had to cross the Pyrénées first… and over there to the west is where we have come from and Rennes-le-Château, to the North is Toulouse and Albi. You know Albi is where the persecution of the Cathars started. That's why it is was called the Albigensian Heresy. That's all I want to say now…so will you play? Tell me what you found?"

"Just a railway ticket," answered Bernard.

"Is that all?" hissed Madeleine "I thought it was something important from Saunière's time."

"It had a note with it which seemed to be by a Senor Balti and said, if my Spanish is good enough, something about finding a connection in Perpignan which held a key to the Saunière mystery. It is signed S. Balti and there is a little drawing of an elephant under the signature. It looks pretty old but obviously it was hidden well after Saunière's time so maybe it belonged to somebody who was interested in Saunière in some way."

"Would you phone me from Perpignan and tell me if you found anything interesting? Here's my card." Bernard noted the address, Dr Diane Jackson, 25 rue Aristide, Quillan, Aude, and carefully inserted it into his wallet.

Bernard looked at Madeleine and they both nodded OK. "If only to calm this American and get on our way," thought Bernard.

"OK kids, now I'll rush you to Perpignan in time for lunch. I'll drop you at a place in the old centre where you can get a great moules frites. They used to have some fast food place in this glorious old Renaissance building, La Loge I think it's called, but now they've got a real smart café with the best washroom in Perpignan in case you want to freshen up."

Later that afternoon, they made for the station, discovering it was at the end of an exotic street of tall palm trees.

"This is the most beautiful street I've ever seen leading to a railway station," remarked Madeleine, gazing up at the tall fronds sharply outlined against a clear blue sky, "and look at that sign...it says 'Au centre de l'univers' and it's pointing to the railway station? C'est curieux. Well what do we do now with your famous ticket?"

"I don't know, but look at that odd looking statue on top of the station. Do you know what it is?"

"Well this is Place Salvador Dalí so it is probably Senor Dalí himself – only he could have inspired such a surreal pose lying backwards with his feet up in the air."

"Did you say Senor Dalí? Do you think the note could have been from him? Senor Balti?"

Bernard fished the note out of his pocket and stared at it. Madeleine looked over Bernard's shoulder.

"Oui I think you have been mistaken! Balti. That B could be a D and that t might be a flourish. So maybe Senor Dalí has brought us to the centre of the universe! But what do you think that could mean?"

"Dalí was a Catalan and lived in Port Lligat which is not far from here over the border, so maybe he used this station...but why the statue, why should he have a place named after him?"

"I don't know but we have to find out. How about a little trip to the tourist office?"

"Oui monsieur, madame?"

The young, dark haired girl looked up from her Paris Match magazine, perhaps dreaming of the boulevards. They told her they were art enthusiasts and were on the trail of anything about Dalí and wondered if she knew of anything about Dalí's special connection with Perpignan.

"It is said that when Dalí visited Perpignan in the

nineteen thirties he had...how do you say it?" The girl shrugged her shoulders in that Gallic way and talked rapidly to Madeleine in French ... "an epiphany moment as he came out of the station. Apparently he proclaimed at Perpignan station 'C'est le centre de l'univers - this is the centre of the universe!' Naturellement we love Dalí for that and erected a statue and called the Place after him!...and we even have special Dalí exhibitions. The next one will be..." But Madeleine and Bernard were already out of the door.

A few minutes later they were walking hurriedly in the back streets of Perpignan, Madeleine suddenly stopped. She was clutching a tourist map of Perpignan which she had grabbed as they exited the Tourist Office.

"Bernard, let's see a bit of Perpignan ...I'd like to see the cathedral, it's just at the end of this street."

The cathedral of St Jean sat serenely in a small, sun soaked square. Topped by a Languedocian metal caged belltower and serenaded by a splashing fountain it was hardly imposing, even modest for a cathedral. Passing into the dark interior they were confronted by the astonishing sight of a huge golden baroque reredos altar which spoke of the wealth of the church and the mad artistry of the genius that carved it three centuries earlier. Angels cavorted brandishing golden trumpets, cupids leapt and saints stared sternly out at the surprised visitors. This conjuration of a vision of paradise suddenly disappeared... the light went out as the last tourist's euro worth of illumination expired.

In near darkness again they stumbled on another

extraordinary thing. A tableau of the severed head of John the Baptist.

"Wow, look at that!" exclaimed Bernard. "This cathedral takes its dedication to St Jean seriously. It's almost like the real thing!"

"Except, according to the Church the real thing is in Amiens Cathedral. I have seen it when I was fifteen. I went on a school trip, they have the skull of John the Baptist there brought back from the Holy Land. It is really weird to see such a thing. I don't know that I believe it really is what they say but you never know. But something much more interesting to me is that the Knights Templar were said to have worshipped a severed head, some think it may have represented John the Baptist or Baphomet, and was one of the reasons that the Pope launched his long night of the knives against them on October 13th 1307."

"My God, you know the exact date!"

Madeleine smiled. "It's only because it's famous because that's where the superstition of Friday the Thirteenth comes from. It was a question in my Baccalaureat!"

"But seriously," she added, "there may be a connection with the Cathars as some say that the treasure of Montségur could have been the treasure brought back from the Holy Land by the Knights Templar."

But Bernard was already lost as she talked on about Cathars and Templar knights. Her words receded into a blur and all he could see was Madeleine's smile lighting up her face. She is so pretty when she smiles, he thought.

"Hey kids, what did you find out?" Diane answered her mobile and found her hijacked couple on the other end. "Why don't you pick up your car and drive over to Rennes-le-Château? I'm volunteering at the museum later so meet me there. I'll be showing some tourists around but we'll have time to chat. Hey, I'm real sorry about what I did. Forgive?" she wheedled.

"Let's hire a car and meet her," urged Madeleine. "It could be really useful if we want to go on with our quest."

A few hours later, standing by the very Visigothic column in which Saunière had discovered the coded papers, Bernard felt he may be about to play a part in unravelling the mystery.

Diane couldn't hide her excitement when they told her about the Dalí discovery.

"OK, now I know why I had to show you that view from Força Réal. I think I get it...the centre of the universe, maybe it's also the centre of Dalí's universe. Let's look at a map... I've got one in the office."

"See, if we draw a line from Perpignan station to Dalí's home in Spain in the south, let's have a look at what happens if we take that line in a radius to mark out a similar distance in other directions from Perpignan. Look at that – we've got, Montségur, Rennes-le-Château in the west and Béziers in the east, Carcassonne in the North."

"It's Cathar country!" exclaimed Madeleine. "Béziers is where the first Cathar massacre happened when the whole town was murdered, even everyone who took sanctuary in the Cathedral. You know what Arnald-Amaury, the Papal legate, said to the soldiers when they asked how they could tell the Catholics from the Cathars? He said, 'Kill them all, God will recognise his own.' Mon Dieu, that gave me mal d'estomac when I first heard it. And in Carcassonne, many Cathars were imprisoned and tortured there. You know, by the notorious inquisitor Bernard Gui." Madeleine looked at Bernard. "You have his name."

"Well I may be a reincarnated Inquisitor if you are a reincarnated Cathar, and we are working out our karma together," Bernard joked.

"Back to business kids," interrupted Diane, "think about Dalí a minute. It's also his universe. He was a Catalan. This area is Catalonia as it was before the separation of French and Spanish Catalonia by the Treaty of the Pyrénées in 1659."

"But where does the station fit into this? Why did he say it at the railway station?"

"I think maybe you should pay a visit to Figueras," suggested Diane, "to visit Dalí's museum. You are bound to find some clue there. Just keep an open mind and wait for insights... that's what I do. Or you could just have a good time together, drink some sangria and eat some paella or something."

"Oui, sounds formidable!" exclaimed Madeleine.

"But I thought you had to get back to Paris?"

"I'll contact my office, ask for a couple more days off... this is too intéressant to leave now."

"And so are you," thought Bernard, torturing himself with

his thoughts turning from mysteries of Cathars and priests to the mysteries of woman. Ah, he sighed inwardly. They can never be understood.

Chapter 4

Paris 1893

Bérenger Saunière felt small in Paris. Compared with the quiet hilltop village of Rennes-le-Château it was bedlam. Carriages clattering over cobblestones, the hubbub of crowds in the streets, the calls of stallholders all added up to a noise level the priest was not used to. He had completed the business part of his trip and had taken the coded documents to the expert at St Sulpice recommended by his Bishop. Relieved of the documents, he was now on his way to the opera. Emma Calvé was appearing in the role which had brought her fame, Carmen, and he could barely contain himself at the thought of seeing the diva who was lionised by the opera goers at the Palais Garnier.

The priest was a robust man in vigorous health but he felt nervous in the throng of well dressed men and elegant, beautiful women. He walked in a euphoric state up the grand staircase, dazzled by the fabulous chandeliers and the sensuous, smooth feel of the curving marble balustrade. He had heard that some of the marble used in building this great foyer even came from Languedoc. His gaze moved from marble glories to the beauty of alabaster white skin as it rested momentarily on the decolletage of a beautiful young woman as she swept passed him. He noted the diamonds at her delicate throat, the swell of her breasts and felt himself flush. This celibate life was not really for him!

Bérenger was transported with delight. Never had he heard such glorious singing, never had he seen such a delightful, talented woman who appeared to be singing to him alone at certain emotional moments. He knew he was imagining this but it exercised his mind as to how he could possibly meet her. Would it be alright to send flowers to her dressing room?

"Monsieur," the gentleman sitting next to him addressed Saunière amidst the thunderous roar of the clapping and the ardent shouts of bravo. "I see that you are really enjoying Mme Calvé and I note that you are maybe new to Paris and the opera?" Bérenger flushed. This sophisticated Parisian had noticed he was out of place here and his sober priest's garb was unusual amongst the suave elegance of the other men. Or perhaps it was his manners that had given him away, his southern accent when yelling bravo?

"Oui monsieur, I am from the country, a small village in the Languedoc, and this is my first visit to Paris and the opera. It is all very exciting for me you understand."

"Monsignor, I am delighted to see you enjoy yourself and would ask you to accompany me, if you are free, to a party which is being held for Mme Calvé at her apartment on the Boulevard Haussmann tomorrow night. I would be honoured to introduce you to more of Parisian life."

Bérenger took the gentleman's card, his hand trembling slightly with excitement. He glanced swiftly at it; Count

Anton Liebowitz, 17 rue de Longchamp.

"Sir I am most grateful... but are you sure? I mean as Mme Calvé does not know me..."

"Nonsense my dear man. Mme Calvé likes to meet new and interesting people and gentlemen who are new converts to the opera and her singing. She is quite vain you know and thrives on a little new adoration, most particularly when it is obviously so genuine as in your case. No sir, put aside any doubts and you will be most welcome. There is something you should know first. I myself am interested in the occult, which is a passion of Emma's too, and tomorrow night there will be a séance. If this is offensive to you, you may not wish to come."

As a priest he knew he should say this was not something he could attend, but he knew that nothing short of supping with the devil himself would prevent him from accepting this wonderful invitation.

"No, no monsieur, I shall be delighted to come and myself am open minded on such matters."

"I will see you at Mme Calvé's, 30 Boulevard Haussmann tomorrow night at 8 then, Monsieur...?

"Saunière, Monsignor Bérenger Saunière."

The count bowed and took his leave. Bérenger stared after him open mouthed with delight and amazement. Surely God has smiled on me tonight, he thought.

The house was an imposing building in one of the richest arrondissements in Paris. Bérenger felt his country origins deeply as he pulled the bell and waited. The footman wearing a haughty expression admitted him when he proffered the card of Count Liebowitz. Everything about the interior conspired to make Bérenger's large bulk diminish slowly until he felt himself to be the size of a six year old child as he entered the salon, which was alive with glittering dresses and elegant gentlemen. The sparkle of champagne served by liveried waiters, the chandeliers, the velvet curtains overawed him. He wanted to turn and run down the sweeping staircase into the street and throw himself into the nearest fiacre cab, but something spurred him on. His ambition, his lust for riches, his desire for the company of beautiful women, his need to know that he, Bérenger Saunière, could share in this glittering panorama of Paris, so far away from his quiet evenings in the company of his housekeeper Marie Dénarnaud at Rennes-le-Château.

As he hesitated, a hand grabbed Bérenger's arm. "Ah Monsignor, you have come. Let me introduce you to Mme Calvé." The count gently steered Bérenger through the crowd which parted like the Red Sea as he was led to another door. "Mme Calvé is in the drawing room with a few of her close friends...they are about to have a séance," whispered the Count in a confidential manner.

Bérenger wondered if he was dreaming as he stood before the beautiful Emma Calvé. "Ah Monsignor Saunière, enchantée." She extended a hand and Bérenger had the presence of mind to raise the bejewelled fingers to his lips and bestow a slightly hurried and embarrassed kiss. "The count has told me you were at the opera for the first time...

and did you enjoy it monsieur?" What followed was even more surprising to Bérenger as his adored Diva took over from the count and introduced him to a small circle of friends as 'my visitor from his charming village in the south.' It was clear to Bérenger that the count had been right in his assessment of Mme Calvé in her fascination with new admirers, and he realised he need not feel anxious about his humble background. It was his newness to the circle of admirers that mattered to Emma. He was careful to lard his conversation with expressions of his admiration for the adored one at the centre of their gathering, but the besotted look on his face was proof enough of his qualifications for admission to this magic circle.

"Attention messieurs et mesdames, please be seated for the séance will begin in a few minutes."

Bérenger was near delirious when he found himself being seated next to Emma. In his awkwardness he began to make the acquaintance of the man on his left. An intense, bearded man with slicked down black hair gazed back at him. Talking to his opposite neighbour the man was saying, "I find our age so singularly ungracious in its ado about less than nothing. We look down our noses quite mistakenly at American bluff, while we produce a kind of artistic bluff which will come home to roost one of these days, what do you think M. Saunière?"

Not used to this level of artistic chatter, Bérenger didn't know what to think let alone what to say in reply. "Well I..." started Bérenger.

Emma clapped her hands. "Now settle down everyone. Mme Blavatsky is ready to begin."

The room was in near darkness and Bérenger could make out the silhouette of Mme Blavatsky as she emitted strange groans which appeared to come from some space he had never heard made vocal before. The first spirit to communicate, appearing as in a white mist, was that of a little boy who claimed to have been murdered by his stepfather and was seeking justice for his soul. The incantation went on interminably with no real conclusion in identifying whom the little spirit wanted to talk to in the room.

"Maybe there is nobody here can help," remarked Mme Blavatsky and waited for an answer, when suddenly another spirit appeared to be talking to her. Her voice changed and Bérenger was listening to the voice of a young woman. She made no bones about it at all and Mme Blavatsky was commanded to draw the initials MM in the spilt sugar on the tablecloth. "Mary Magdalene!" Madame exclaimed as she continued lurching from one voice to the other. MM, for it was truly she, said she had been drawn to the séance because of the presence of a parish priest from the south of France. Bérenger started in his chair and felt his heart beat faster. "Mon Dieu, c'est moi Madame!"

"Monsignor, I wish you to ask for the Secret to be told to you by the gentleman sitting next to you and then go home and dedicate your church to me and build a tower which should overlook the plain of Razès." With that the voice got fainter and Mary Magdalene had returned to whereof she came.

Bérenger turned to M. Debussy. "Did that mean anything to you, monsieur?"

"Yes. I have to tell you I am as shocked as you are, you are trembling sir, but I know too well what the Magdalene meant. It is just such a surprise that she should demand that I share the Secret with, excuse me Sir, a mere parish priest. Come and see me tomorrow at my home and I will tell you something which may turn your hair white."

The Secret did very nearly turn Bérenger's hair white, it certainly terrified him. M. Debussy, apart from being a prominent and popular composer, announced himself to Bérenger as also Grand Master of an organisation called the Priory of Sion which he described as a secret society dedicated to guarding a great secret which would shake the world. M. Debussy told Bérenger that there was a Gospel of Mary Magdalene, which had been suppressed at the Council of Nicaea, in which Jesus's close relationship with Mary Magdalene was hinted at. He preferred her to all the other disciples and would often kiss her on the mouth.

"There is a repressed Gospel of Philip where the relationship between Jesus and Mary is openly discussed. The male disciples asked why do you love her more than us? And he replied, 'Why do I not love you like her? Great is the mystery of marriage – for without it the world would not have existed.'

"Jesus and Mary Magdalene were married at the wedding at Cana in the year AD30 when she was 27. Mary became Jesus's wife that day. Only as a bride and a priestess in her own right would Mary have the right to anoint his head and feet with the sacred ointment spikenard as she famously did. She conceived in December AD32 and bore her daughter Tamar."

"Thus Monsignor you see the origin of the Bloodline of the Holy Grail was indeed the womb of Mary Magdalene."

"But why have I been given this secret?" stuttered Bérenger as he felt his nervous tic causing him to tremble again.

"You know that the most active Magdalene cult was established in the Languedoc in your very own village of Rennes-le-Château. It is here that since 1059 when your church was dedicated to her that the cult of Mary Magdalene flourished. It is not now so strange that the Magdalene chose to appear to you at the séance... and no doubt your excellent honest character can be trusted with information which may destroy another man. I think the Magdalene knows that you have a deep reverence for her and your church is in the Languedoc area where the Magdalene herself landed at Saintes Maries de la Mer when she fled to France after the crucifixion."

"Monsieur, I would like to return with you to your church and look around for myself, and if you permit me I will bring Mme Calvé with me as she was much excited by what happened last night."

Bérenger was only too happy to agree to this unexpected delight – the presence of his adored one in Rennes seemed like an impossible piece of luck which could only be attributed to the Divine Presence smiling on him in Paris!

"I am truly amazed but less surprised than I should be by your revelation monsieur. I came to Paris with encoded documents which I found in my church. At the behest of my Bishop I visited the church of St Sulpice where I have had help from the learned priest there. He advised me to go to the Louvre where I purchased prints of a painting by Nicolas Poussin which I am sure has the countryside of Rennes in the background. It has been dawning on me that Rennes is in some way connected with some great secret which is being passed on to me, first by my chance discovery of the documents when refurbishing my church, secondly by the help received at St Sulpice and now by the surprising intervention of Mary Magdalene at the seance!"

"You may not be surprised then monsieur," M. Debussy replied, "if I tell you that Nicolas Poussin was also a Grand Master and therefore one of the custodians of the Secret."

Abbé Bérenger Saunière

Chapter 5

Rennes-le-Château 1893

Several weeks later Bérenger Saunière sent a horse and carriage to meet the little train which was due in at Couiza station carrying the formidable duo of Emma Calvé and Claude Debussy to his remote part of the world. With few of the luxuries that they were used to, Bérenger worried about how they would enjoy the poor circumstance of a country priest's living and the humble surroundings that a hilltop village offered compared to the grand boulevards and fashionable cafés of Paris.

The villagers turned to stare in disbelief as the elegant satin shoe of Emma Calvé emerged first from the carriage door, followed by a swish of silk as she gathered her skirts to step onto the muddy road outside the priest's house. Marie, the housekeeper, drew the lace curtain aside enough to stare at the visitors. "Painted harlot," she whispered to herself and, as the priest raised Emma's smooth little hand to his pouting mouth, Marie spat out "Parisienne!" Monsieur Debussy was regarded a little more favourably by Marie as she served the steaming wild boar dinner that evening. Handsome and charming, she felt less hostile to him, but one look at his clothes showed he was obviously wealthy and from Paris and didn't belong here with honest country people.

What is Father up to inviting these grand people to

Rennes? It was probably to do with the excavations and those papers he had found she mused. Marie had been housekeeper for Father Bérenger since she was a young girl and regarded him proprietorially, and certainly resented the presence of another woman in the house, particularly one who was so obviously glamorous and seductive as Emma Calvé. She was even wearing a low cut gown which showed too much of her bosom. Well she'd heard that these fine Parisiennes were not much better than prostitutes! A famous opera singer! She'd make her sing a different tune if she had half a chance.

During their stay M. Debussy was completely enchanted by the little village and claimed he could psychically sense the esoteric powers lying in the landscape. "Right beneath my feet Father!" he exclaimed as he excitedly stamped on the rocky ground near the edge of the hill on which Rennes stood. "This is where you must build a tower and dedicate it to Mary Magdalene. It will survey this great landscape where the Visigothic kingdom of Razès once was and where Siegebert, who established the Merovingian line of Kings, established his Kingdom."

"What is the significance of that to Mary Magdalene?" inquired Bérenger as he shifted his feet on the ground, which had suddenly taken on a holy aura.

"The Merovingians were part of the Bloodline of the Holy Grail, of Jesus and Mary's bloodline!" exclaimed M. Debussy with passion in his voice. Bérenger felt his pulse quicken and wondered again at the extraordinary destiny he had found in Rennes. His own native land, the very area where he was born and played as a child was now revealed as a truly Holy Place. Debussy announced that he had to return to Paris on the train in the morning, having completed what he had come for. However he would be privileged to be allowed to give a little concert on Father Bérenger's piano if he would grant permission.

That evening after another of Marie's copious Languedoc dishes, Boles de Picolat accompanied by a rough but pleasant wine from the region, Debussy wondered why all the Languedoc recipes were dark brown and unappetising to look at, but he nevertheless enjoyed the hearty food which seemed to give him new energy. After musing to himself in this way he suddenly thought of a gift he could give his generous host. He would give the first performance of his newest piece here, not in a salon in Paris as he had intended. He sat at the polished keyboard of the priest's upright piano and played his lyrical music, which quite softened Marie's heart.

"What is it called sir?" she tentatively inquired.

"I don't know, I have just completed it, what do you think?"

"It makes me feel dreamy sir, like when I look at the moon, there's a full moon tonight!"

"That's it Marie!" exclaimed M. Debussy. "Clair de Lune!" Emma, to Bérenger's delight, even rapture, offered to sing and gave her stunning performance of an aria from Carmen. So magnificent was her voice and so strange was it to hear in the humble surroundings that even Marie felt herself melt somewhat towards the Diva and joined in enthusiastically with the clapping of the little audience.

Emma smiled and curtsied graciously before them just as she would do at the Palais Garnier Opéra in Paris. Emma had no immediate need to return to Paris and decided to stay on to enjoy the relaxation of the country air – "it is good for my voice" – for a few more days.

Debussy left Rennes in an elevated mood and thanked Bérenger for being worthy of entrusting the Secret to and told him that Emma already knew and was a loyal follower of the Magdalene cult.

Thrown on each other's company Bérenger was happy to be in her presence. She often accompanied him on walks into the countryside and she showed an amazing, to him, interest in the wildlife and history of the area. "You know Monsignor, you seem a little surprised that I should be enjoying these country pleasures away from fashionable Paris but it was not always so. My childhood was spent in Spain where my father was an engineer, you see not an artist at all, and I remember the happiest times of my life were spent in Spain and in the countryside around Roquefort in France."

On one of these walks where the priest listened enchanted to Emma's tales, they were caught in the rain and had to run back to the house for shelter. In no time they were both helpless with mirth. They had become soaking wet and she found it very funny that her elegant Parisian dress was muddy and wet and her lovely coiffed hair straggly in the rain. When the merriment subsided they found themselves standing

Emma Calvé

closer and looking into each other's eyes. Without warning Bérenger's emotions overwhelmed him and he drew her to him and planted a kiss on her mouth. He withdrew in horror expecting a tirade but instead she drew him back and kissed him passionately. The moon came up and hovered like Debussy's music over the Rennes landscape and lit up the scene taking place in the priest's bedroom.

A curious passer-by may have been surprised that night to see the shadows of two people moving behind the curtains of the priest's villa. Bérenger lifted up Emma's muddied Parisian skirt and, marvelling at the quality of the fabric under his touch, stroked the white silk stockings underneath. She loosed her dark tresses and shook them like an excited mare as she began to remove her corset and free her bosom from its confines. She liked the touch of his rough hands on the delicate skin of her breasts, and feeling his excitement rise with every touch returned his passionate kisses with the ardour of a woman who has known many lovers. When the moment was suddenly there he knew why the church found this so dangerous...a man could spend his days doing nothing else but loving a woman, and when the final moment came it was like he had always imagined it to be, like entering paradise. Years of suppressed lust and longing leapt from his loins into this beautiful woman whom he held in his arms. Bérenger heard the angels sing.

After Bérenger had fallen asleep, Emma lay awake musing about herself and what had just happened. She had many lovers in Paris, mostly young men with riches who had fallen for her and dined her on champagne at Maxim's and Le Pré Catalan in the Bois de Boulogne. She often allowed a quick kiss or an embrace in the back of a hansom cab but usually kept them waiting for weeks or even months before she allowed them to make love to her. Coquettishness was in her nature and she kept the eager young men tantalised until they felt more and more passionate about her. And tonight she had given herself to this portly parish priest at the first kiss! How had this rough and unsophisticated fellow who had none of the charm or manners of her usual lovers, conquered her so quickly? Was it because of his innocence, because they were breaking a taboo or could it be because of his connection with the mystery of Mary Magdalene which she knew Debussy had enlightened him on? Was it this willingness to be the Sacred Feminine for a man who knew the secret that overcame her evasive manner in matters of love?

As the sun woke him from his slumber with the naked Emma in his arms, Bérenger felt a rush of guilt. He had broken his vow of celibacy – and yet this love was so powerful, such a marvellous gift of joy. Surely Our Lord would forgive him? Emma was more matter of fact, assuring him that it was the bringing back of the secret of the Sacred Feminine through the knowledge about Mary Magdalene that could release him from the church's draconian exclusion of sexuality in the life of the priest. She also sowed the idea in his mind that a vow of celibacy was not a vow of chastity. And what priest did not suffer terrible torments which interfered with his pastoral life because of this edict? However, Bérenger was not to be released that easily from the pangs of a tortured conscience, and the conflict between his love for Emma and his obedience to the church tormented his soul.

And then there was the practical issue of how to hide this from Marie. He knew that Marie was secretly in love with him and was completely devoted to him. The priest had often suffered from unassuaged desire when seeing her young girl's body as she moved about the house or, occasionally, getting a glimpse of her breasts as she leaned over him to serve the soup, but he had always resisted the ultimate temptation. And now he had yielded to a woman with a far more dangerous and exotic sexuality! Fortunately Marie had been visiting her mother yesterday and wasn't due back until midday. Meanwhile Emma needed to go back to her room. She gave Bérenger a last passionate kiss and wrapping a sheet around her nakedness slipped out of the room. Emma left for Paris the next day, going back to her fashionable life and rehearsals for a new opera but carrying strangely disturbing emotions stirred by the rough and robust priest.

Bérenger, desolate after her departure, mooched off into the countryside until coming across a rushing stream he sat down on a rock. Picking up a sharp stone he used it to carve a heart and the words EMMA CALVÉ. Covering it with leaves he believed it to be safe from view but somewhere he could come and be with her when the loneliness was too oppressive. As he sat there he noticed the tomb which he had seen in the Poussin painting in the Louvre. Sure enough the countryside of Rennes was reflected in the painting Et in Arcadia Ego! And this was Arques, so nearly Arcadia! This was a kind of Arcadian landscape and suddenly he knew where to look for the treasure. It was where love lies buried as Mary Magdalene had been buried from the church's view for all these centuries. He hurried back to church and began with spade and pick axe to dig at the stone slab under the altar. Excitedly, with sweat pouring down his brow, he thrust his hands into the earth but there was nothing there. Despair overtook him as he had lost his Emma and his dream of finding the treasure where he knew it should be both at the same time. Weeks went by, he spent his time wondering how he could build the tower without the necessary funds and taking little walks to retrace his time with Emma, usually ending up by the tomb at Arques and the carved name which, each time he uncovered, dimmed his vision with tears.

Cadaques, Spain

Chapter 6

Catalan Spain 2004

The remarkable Catalan coast was their leave taking of France; the Côte Vermeille chequered with vineyards on steep hills almost falling into the sea and cultivating some of the best wines of Languedoc. Collioure – a magic little cove and harbour once host to the 'wild beast' artist Matisse whose brilliant colours had captured the exotic little jewel and made it his own. They stopped for lunch at the Copacabana restaurant overlooking the sea and watched the painters doing their obligatory view of the Bell Tower made famous by Matisse.

Madeleine leaned close to Bernard and whispered in his ear "Here is a little story you haven't heard Mister Englishman...a famous French philosopher has seen in the geography of this harbour the body of a woman... and the bell tower is how do you say, the male principle. Or as your famous Dalí called it, the Catalan Phallus! Oui c'est vrai et très Freudian but the whole of Collioure is a metaphor érotique."

Over the border into Spain the very air seemed to change. The Pyrénées, that great barrier between France and Spain since 1685 when the Treaty of the Pyrénées ceded Pyrénées Orientales to France, had made sure that the two countries would always be uniquely themselves.

They checked into the hotel Meson Castilla, nearest the beach, a baroque white building with a statue of Dalí in view from the first floor. Their rooms were next to each other and, like Noel Coward's Private Lives, they were neighbours on their balconies looking out over the Mediterranean.

"It's amazing, this hotel has a collection of Dalí memorabilia and we've just walked right into it!"

The next morning the hotel owner presented himself. "I am Juan Ortega, this is my hotel, I hope you like your stay here. You like Dalí? I saw you looking at my Dalí pieces. I have these from Senor Dalí himself. When I was young I spent a lot of time at the house with Dalí and Gala and his band of followers. Come and see my private collection."

Senor Ortega was himself something of a Daliesque vision, an elegant man in his sixties in a white suit, flowing locks down to his shoulders, but lacking the famous moustache on his smooth shaven upper lip. One could imagine him at the Master's dining table or even lounging on Mae West's lips sofa. He led the way to a little room hidden behind a thick curtain and revealed a treasure house of surreal painting and objets which would have been envied by the curator of any Dalí museum.

"I show these only to people who I know," he smiled mischievously, "are true Dalí aficionados."

"Regardez ça! The elephant!" exclaimed Madeleine, pointing to a small maquette of an elephant with an obelisk on its back. "Didn't Diane say something about Hannibal crossing the Pyrénées near here? Maybe there is a connection with the elephants in Dalí's art."

"No es possible, Dalí always had the ideas from his dreams," protested Senor Ortega.

"Senor Ortega," Madeleine engaged him with her most charming smile, and decided to confide in him. "We are researching Dalí's possible interest in the Rennes-le-Château mystery so we are particularly, how do you say, intéressés in the esoteric side of Dalí's interests which maybe he shows somehow in his art."

"Ah, I do not follow such things myself but then you must meet my wife. She is an art historian at Barcelona University and also has an interest in the esoteric."

Senora Ortega turned out to be not only interested in esoterica but a keen flamenco dancer. And so it was that Madeleine and Bernard found themselves invited to dinner at the hotel's restaurant where Rosita would that night be performing with flamenco dancers.

The flame of flamenco burned hot that night. At the Restaurant Surrealismo their table was practically on the stage, the stamping feet, the flaring scarlet and black dresses, the machismo males, the plaintive cries of the singer brought the audience to a peak of empathic delight. Rosita, one of the two female stars of this performance, was magnificent to watch. Her black hair tightly drawn back to frame a beautiful face with fine bone structure and arching eyebrows, her full skirt flared provocatively. She danced the passion in her soul as she stamped erotically, confronting the proud male dancer who, hands aloft and feet stamping pursued her around the

Flamenco

little stage.

"You like?" whispered Ortega obviously proud of his lovely young wife.

"Oh yes, oui, fantastique, great!" chorused the two guests at Senor Ortega's table.

"More wine? Champagne! Bring a bottle of the best champagne," demanded the host to the attentive waiter.

Two bottles of Dom Perignon later, Bernard felt he was having one of the best nights of his life. But there was more to come.

Rosita sat down and grasped a glass of champagne eagerly. Juan introduced his friends and explained their mission.

"We loved your dancing, extraordinaire!"

"Gracias."

Bernard was entranced by the Spanish beauty whose fiery dancing had affected him. It appeared that Madeleine was similarly affected as she flirtatiously held his hand under the table, squeezed it and asked for "more champagne" as she held her glass unsteadily and hiccoughed ever so slightly, smiling as she did so. He leant over and kissed her bare shoulder. "Vous êtes très charmant ce soir."

"Thank you milord," she whispered as she nuzzled closer and leant on his shoulder.

"Back to business," he whispered as he turned to Rosita and told her of the discovery at Rennes-le-Château and their theory about Dalí's connection.

"You know, I think the elephant is important. Dalí did many sculptures but many are of elephants with an obelisk on their back. I have been researching some of the unconscious symbolism in the work of Renaissance artists and I discovered that Dalí was not the only one to use this symbol, Bernini used it too… in a statue which stands outside the Church Sopra Minerva in Rome."

"Qu'est ce que c'est?"

"I am not sure but I think it is something to do with manifesting Divine Wisdom."

"Wow, we are on to something!" exclaimed Bernard. "The Divine Wisdom and Saunière's receiving special knowledge about the bloodline of the Holy Grail."

"Where do you think this leads?" asked Madeleine.

"Rome!"

That night they didn't attempt to go to their separate rooms. Slightly drunkenly Madeleine wrestled with the key in her lock and pulled Bernard in after her. Their mouths met as they walked backwards to the bed and fell on it in a wild embrace. Between kisses Bernard surfaced long enough to say, "Je t'aime."

Madeleine whispered in his ear, "Moi aussi mon chéri."

They made love with all the enthusiasm of new lovers. Bernard was overwhelmed at the realisation that his lover was the stuff of his once youthful dreams, a beautiful French woman.

They were almost too late for breakfast the next morning. "Were we a metaphor érotique last night?" asked Bernard with a smile.

"Mon chéri, pas metaphor c'etait vraiment l'amour!"

Chapter 7

Rome 2004

As he stood at the foot of the Spanish Steps, Bernard found the memory of that film from the fifties with Audrey Hepburn returning to his mind. Roman Holiday had, he soon discovered, become an iconic emblem for Rome as its many news kiosks flaunted a still from the movie with Hepburn and Gregory Peck alongside its souvenir maps of ancient Rome. Anyway this holiday was not going to be so romantic as he was now alone wistfully remembering Madeleine and their farewell night. No need tonight for the eager rose sellers on the Spanish Steps, he thought.

Madeleine had returned to her office in Paris and yet he had felt impelled to continue the journey of discovery...to discover what? He didn't really know but the fascination of the search had him in its grip. He had to see the Colosseum, the Forum and the Pantheon before he did anything else and, in any case, doing the obvious tourist things may lead him to something unexpected. Tired after an exhaustive exploration of ancient Rome he sat with a sigh of relief on the terrace of a café opposite the Pantheon. He ordered what was billed in his guide book as the best iced coffee in Rome. Reading on from this excellent recommendation he discovered that the church of the Santa Maria Sopra Minerva which Rosita had talked about was just a few steps away.

Sure enough there was the elephant and it did have an obelisk on its back. It stood outside the church on an intimate little Roman piazza. Inside Bernard was astonished to find a fabulous Gothic interior bursting with angels, glorious frescoes by Fra Filippo Lippi and vaulted Gothic arches so unlike anything he had seen in Rome and almost belonging in northern Europe.

A tiny monkish man approached him. "Is very nice church. Is only mediaeval gothic church in Rome. You like guide Signor?" Bernard's instinct was to say no and see it for himself but he reminded himself that he needed information which a guide may have.

"Yes, I would be pleased to hear about this church," he answered. The little monk pointed out the Michaelangelo statue of Christ carrying his cross. Bernard thought it wasn't the best Michaelangelo he had seen but it did seem to express in Christ's gaze his regret at leaving the world. The monk grabbed at the sleeve of Bernard's linen jacket as he eagerly pulled him in the direction of an imposing looking tomb.

"Guarda, look here is buried Saint Dominic. He begin the Dominicans and is famous for his put down of heretics," said the monk.

"Heretics!" exclaimed Bernard. "Would that include the Cathars?"

"Si, Catholics who not good believers," replied the little man grimacing disapprovingly at the thought of dissenters.

"No, I mean the Cathars, the 13th century sect who were

dualists in France and Italy," explained Bernard as he looked agitatedly at the tomb of the arch enemy of the Good Men.

"Non so," replied the monk baffled by the Englishman's use of a strange word, Cathers? Pity these northern European Protestants were not put down too by St Dominic, he mused.

Bernard remembered that 140 Cathars had been burnt in Minerve in the Languedoc after Simon de Montfort's attack on the town. Was it a coincidence that this church was named too after the goddess Minerva?

What about the elephant? Would this little monk know anything interesting about that? "Ah, il elephant, si, it is made by the great Bernini."

"And the obelisk, that is odd isn't it putting that there?"

"Not to Bernini. He was great Master of Spiritual knowledge. He entrusted the knowledge to the curators of the Sopra Minerva and it has been kept right up to this day. The elephant is the great earth beast who funnels the Divine Wisdom from the mystical obelisk pointing to the heavens. Only a strong mind can endure the weight of the Divine Wisdom," added the monk, pointing to the quotation in the guide book.

Bernard produced from his pocket a photo of the sculpture of Dali's elephant and obelisk. "Would you say the artist Salvador Dalí had a strong mind, Signor?" The elderly monk started as if he had been pricked. "Signor, do you know why Dalí made this sculpture?"

"Many years ago Signor Dalí come here, I was a young man then and he take big interest like you in the Bernini statue. I not know he copy it!" he said, looking disapprovingly at the photograph.

"Did he tell you why he was so interested?".

The monk shrugged his shoulders and drew away as if he wanted to get rid of this inquisitive tourist. "Let me think, well I remember something about he received the divine wisdom from the elephant and the obelisk in a dream after his first visit here."

"Dalí had great messages from his unconscious mind in his dreams which always inspired his art," added Bernard.

The monk, however, was lost in his memory of the encounter with the great Spanish eccentric whose morals he was not at all sure about – wasn't he called the Great Masturbator? "Dalí tell me about treasure he was looking for and the two places in Rome which could lead to it, one was Santa Maria Sopra Minerva and the other was... what was it? mmm, begins with a 'T' I think Trajan's Column? Trastevere? Tiber? No, not these." A pause and he pronounced triumphantly, "Titus Arch!"

Later from the comfort of lying on the bed in his hotel room after a revitalising shower in the marble bathroom, Bernard phoned Madeleine.

"Allo," a female voice replied backed by a cacophony of noise.

"Where are you?"

"Dining at La Coupole in Montparnasse with a client," she whispered. He heard her make a whispered exchange. And soon the noise disappeared. "OK I can talk now but better not be too long," she said. "How are you? I miss you and wish I was in Rome. It would be nice to be with you now."

"Miss you too, you could be in my mental movie of a Roman Holiday. You'd be a lovely Audrey Hepburn, with French style of course."

"And you would be a nice Gregory Peck but maybe I recast you English man as that charming David Niven."

"Who is your client?"

"Oh makes cheeps."

"Cheeps? What's that?"

"Cheeps, you eat, for snack."

"CHIPS!"

"Oui, cheeps, maybe you call them crisps I think." The noise of the restaurant drowned out the last sentence and Bernard was left wondering what chips you would eat as a snack.

Bernard quickly recounted what he had found out in the Sopra Minerva church. When he got to the discovery of the Dominican connection with the Inquisition he heard a loud exclamation from Madeleine – "Poof! Yesterday I had this visitation from Esclarmonde who tell me about her friend Pierre Clergue who was tortured by the Inquisition. She cursed Dominic but most particularly the inquisitor Bernard Gui who led the torture on the thing that pull you."

"Rack."

"I must tell you all about Esclarmonde but now I go back to the table or my client will wonder what is keeping me so long."

"Is he good looking, your client?"

"Very good looking, you could say very beautiful to look at! He is a woman! Stop being jealous and you can come to Paris and see me after you have finished in Rome and we can have a fun weekend together before you take the Eurostar to London."

Bernard lay back on the bed in his white bathrobe. She had a visitation from Esclarmonde! From seven centuries ago! What an amazing woman! Looking at the elephant in the guide book he had purchased at Sopra Minerva, Bernard suddenly understood – the obelisk was a marker and it marked the inquisition of the Cathars - by Dominic! Presumably Dalí knew that Bernini had coded this information into his statue to mark the fact that it was the Cathars who had the Divine Wisdom, not the Inquisitor Dominic, so Dalí had used the same symbol to lead searchers from Rennes-le-Château to this place. With a sigh of relief his thoughts turned back to Madeleine and Paris. Tomorrow he would go and look at The Arch of Titus.

Strolling through Rome proved to meet Bernard's every expectation of the Eternal City. He passed a shop on the Via Condotti which sold nothing but priest's vestments, another which sold wooden dolls of Pinocchio, ice cream carts decorated with kitsch paintings of the Colosseum and St Peters and the Fontane de Trevi evoking memories of Anita Ekberg in La Dolce Vita. How he wished Madeleine were here to share it with him. Instead he phoned her on his mobile, got a voice mail and left a message saying he was throwing three coins in for them to return together. Sipping his hot, sweet and delicious espresso ("just like a kiss should be"), he studied his Michelin Green Guide and all it had to say about the Forum.

Later, strolling around the Forum in the hot sun he was overawed by the state of the ruins. He had no idea it would be possible to reconstruct in his mind's eye some of the remarkable buildings he knew so well from studying old drawings of their probable original form. His imagination was racing back 2000 years, hardly daring to believe he was in the very place where Caesar, Augustus and Mark Anthony trod the ground where he stood. And finally there it was, the Arch of Titus. Squinting in the bright sunlight, Bernard could make out the outline of a candelabra, with seven branches. The famous Menorah from the Treasure of Solomon which legend says Titus brought back from the Holy Land. He climbed a few steps and found himself on Capitoline Hill and a marvellous statue of the philosopher Emperor Marcus Aurelius. Standing by the statue on Michaelangelo's piazza, Bernard suspected that these two geniuses of the human spirit would urge him to be patient and take a break from the physical search and await help from more traditional sources.

The Green Guide yielded no more information but later that day Bernard pored over volumes of histories of Rome in the main library. After two or three hours of exhausting reading he discovered an entry which claimed that Alaric, the leader of the Visigoth tribes who sacked Rome in 410, carried the treasure of the ransacked city away to the Visigothic kingdom of Razès in the Languedoc. Razès! A delighted smile spread over Bernard's face, the location of Rennes-le-Château!

So Dalí had led him here to this arch via the Perpignan railway station allusion to it being the centre of the universe. Dalí's universe stretched from his home in Port Lligat to Minerve where 180 Cathars were burnt at the stake, in the North, to Béziers in the West where Simon de Montfort massacred all the Cathars in the town, to Rennes-le-Château in the east where the mystery of the Magdalene linked with the Cathars. Perhaps, he thought, secrets which could lead to a hidden treasure were buried or encoded in manuscripts by the Cathars themselves or others who had inherited the Secret.

Dalí had inhabited this mental universe and ensured that he would lead a true enquirer to find his way to the Arch through his obsessive sculptures, drawings and even jewellery depicting the elephant carrying an obelisk on its back. The elephant of Hannibal crosses the Alps once again to find its true home in Rome. Bernard drew in a sharp breath as he realised that the elephant and the obelisk were also connected with the inquisition of the Cathars. Dalí's elephant had led him to Sopra Minerva where St Dominic, the prosecutor of the inquisition was buried! My God, Dalí was not only a surrealist painter. He had a surreal mind when planning this complicated game of following the clues he had left! But maybe I have been sent a little mad by Dalí's mind, wondered Bernard. If this is true it is really fantastic but I need to get another view and I can't think of anyone better to go over it all with than Madeleine. He resolved to take her up on her invitation and catch a plane to Paris for that promised weekend. And soon he was thinking of other things than Cathars and crazy surrealist painters.

She was waiting for him at the airport and, giving him a kiss on the cheek, grabbed his arm to lead him to her waiting car. "Well, have you found anything in Rome?"

"Have I!" He told her of the Titus Arch and how it all connected up to Dali's elephant clues and led to the Menorah stolen from Jerusalem and ending up in Rennes-le-Château. "And what was that nonsense you were telling me about seeing Esclarmonde?" asked Bernard with a wry smile.

"Pas de nonsense!" she exclaimed. "I really felt her and she speak to me about the knowledge that the Cathars had that Catharism would return in 700 years...and that is now M. le Smartaleck. Maintenant, this is why she was looking for a woman like her from this century to communicate with and so she find me and she appear when I was nearly asleep in that little space between being awake and asleep...psychologists call it hypnogogic, but anyway it's ideal for a spirit to get through to someone who is a sensitive and a believer like me.

"And then when I went to sleep I had this strange dream in which I was at one of the Cathar castles, Château Puivert I think. That's the castle where the troubadours were... I saw troubadours playing such beautiful music to their ladies which they kept calling mon Dompa. What do you think that means?"

"I have no idea, and anyway you said this bit was a dream so you need Freud not me."

"Well, anyway it was a marvellous dream ... this lady came to me, oh she was so beautiful and her dress! No wonder we French are so good at fashion, it must have started back then... and I knew instantly that the troubadours and many of the ladies were Cathars too and that the worshipping of their lady, which of course the troubadours practised without ever going to bed with them, was really the manifestation of the Sacred Feminine which had come from the Magdalene cult in the Languedoc."

Bernard all the time was thrilled to be careering through Paris, past the boulangeries and the pavement cafés until Madeleine exclaimed, "Nous sommes arrivés" as they turned into rue de Moscou. "Here is my flat".

After parking she entered the code and pushed open the heavy door, greeted the concierge and pressed the bell for the lift. They entered the smallest metal cage Bernard had ever seen. They were pressed together and Bernard pulled him to her over his bulky case and kissed her passionately as the cage groaned its upward journey. The journey was sadly short as it clanked to a halt on the second floor and they squeezed out.

"What are you doing Bernard? Worshipping the Sacred Feminine?"

They lay in Madeleine's bateau lit bed. "You are merveilleuse, chérie," whispered Bernard as he caressed her ear lobe.

"Merci monsieur, and you, you are not like Englishman at all! You know one of our ex prime ministers, Edith Cresson, say all Englishmen are homosexual or don't know how to appreciate a woman. I have just proved her wrong!"

"Now tell me more about Esclarmonde's appearance," urged Bernard.

"So you believe me now eh? Alors, she show me this picture of a torture which took place in Canet en Roussillon. A Pierre Dutois, the blacksmith was tortured in front of his wife by the Inquisition. They say that the blacksmith must have been a Cathar protected by the Devil because he was the only one to survive an outbreak of the plague in the town. But he didn't catch the plague because the noise of his anvil kept the rats away – they hate noise."

"OK, I believe you mon Dompa," he whispered in her ear. Madeleine sensed that Esclarmonde was around her still as she felt herself drawn to Bernard as Esclarmonde was drawn to her troubadour admirer. She knew she was a template for strange emotions from another time and era but Madeleine was living in both at once.

Through her attraction to Bernard she was more open and receptive to the secrets that were being revealed to her by Esclarmonde; the secrets of the Sacred Feminine and the Cathar mysteries.

"Not your Dompa, just me – and maybe Esclarmonde. You know Esclarmonde means Light of the World," she replied smiling.

"OK, I believe you mon Dompa," he whispered in her ear.

Chapter 8

Antoine Rings the Bells 1894

It was a Sunday just after mass when the bellringer, Antoine, suddenly appeared by the priest's side. Young Antoine had recently taken over from his father, Jules Cordier, whose arthritic hands now prevented him from ever again pulling on the great bell rope.

"Monsignor, there is something I have to tell you. It has been weighing on my mind and it is too big a thing for a modest man such as myself."

"What is it Antoine, speak up!"

"In that pillar which supports the pulpit, where you have just been preaching to the parishioners about their sins and so on, but I wouldn't say they was so much sins as little foibles that we all have, your reverence, and as for myself I don't think it's really a sin to just look at a pretty girl and have thoughts is it?"

"Now Antoine, let's say it's probably not too bad a sin and tell me about this pillar." The priest's hand rested on the pillar and began stroking it.

"If you go on touching a bit harder sir that'll just come away as it's a loose bit and behind it there's a little glass phial with something in it like a document of some sort." Antoine paused for breath after this outburst and noticed the strange look in the priest's eyes.

Sure enough Antoine was right. How had he overlooked this? It wasn't as if he hadn't touched the pillar every day of his life. Holding the little phial in his hand he thought this is from inside an old Visigothic pillar so perhaps Antoine has stumbled on something.

"It's probably nothing at all important, probably just a sermon left by a previous priest so he could pick it up as he went to the pulpit." Apparently dismissive, he plunged it into his cassock pocket and began to talk about the bell ringing which Antoine had been doing lately. "It needs a bit more of a dong after the ding Antoine," he said. Antoine scratched his head and scampered up the tower to try and see what the priest meant. After a few practice dings and dongs he smiled with pleasure at the result. The priest was right, he thought, and rushed down to seek out the priest's opinion on his new ringing. Monsignor was nowhere to be seen and he had forgotten to put the broken bit of pillar back. Antoine shoved it back crossly murmuring "priests" and thinking of that pretty young girl who had smiled at him yesterday at the market in Esperaza. I wonder, thought Antoine.

After wrestling with what the strange little document said (it appeared to be written in Occitan which he didn't know). Saunière searched out his friend Jacques St Cyr, a scholar at the University of Carcassonne, and asked him over to dinner one night. After Marie had served the Muscat de Rivesaltes at the end of the dinner Bérenger turned the conversation to the work that Jacques did in recovering old Occitan writings and casually mentioned his little find and asked Jacques for his opinion. Jacques was very keen on researching old documents so he was more than delighted to be asked.

"Just let's keep what we find to ourselves though Jacques, as it's really church property and I'd have to clear it with the Vatican before we could tell anyone about its contents."

The Vatican! Jacques stroked his little goatee beard thoughtfully. "The Cathars used to put up with a lot from the Vatican so as I'm a bit of a Cathar myself, do you know, with due respect to the church today, I wonder if they didn't have something in that dualism idea and the way they thought that men and women were equal. I know you wouldn't get burned for saying so today but there's far too much power in the hands of us men. Women have a lot to offer society too, there sir that's my opinion! I'm not too keen on anything I work on getting into the hands of the Vatican."

It didn't take Jacques long to realise that the scrap of paper was a map indicating where certain Visigothic kings and warriors were buried – and the location of the burial ground was just outside of Rennes. Why in Occitan he didn't know but Jacques wondered whether it was written in Cathar times and hidden because of the Inquisition. Well the Cathars knew many secrets and it wouldn't be surprising if this was yet another one of them.

"Merveilleux, merveilleux!" he uttered as he went out clutching the priest's hand in a fierce handshake. "Merveilleux," the priest heard him murmuring it still as he disappeared into his carriage and rode home.

Jacques hadn't been gone long when Bérenger enlisted Marie to get a spade and come with him. It was a moonlit night. It reminded Marie of the charming man from Paris and his little song. Privy to all the priest's secrets except one, she went out with him into the night. For several nights they searched by candlelight and dug at various sites but only found a few scraps of metal which may have belonged to some warrior's armour or maybe not. On the seventh night when they were exhausted and dispirited, Bérenger hit something hard with his spade. They set to furiously digging with their hands when the spade wouldn't do, and with sweat dripping down their brows, dragged out a metal container.

Bérenger and Marie dragged and pulled the metal box out of the ground and carrying it between them stumbled towards the house with anticipation and fear. Fear of what they might find, fear of what they might not find. They couldn't wait until the morning, even in their state of exhaustion they attacked the rusting case with various tools which Marie had suddenly assembled.

Marie wiped away a tear of frustration caused partly by the task in hand, partly by the realisation she had earlier in the day when she remembered the way Bérenger and that woman looked at each other, remembered Emma's unslept in bed on the day she had left the villa. Marie knew, but was only now admitting to herself that she really knew, that he and the opera singer were lovers. Shame on him for doing such a thing but that he had never succumbed to her passionate young body when she had tried over the years to arouse his ardour. That was what really hurt.

"Marie! It's opening, it's opening!" All other thoughts were swept aside as they both witnessed the glint of gold. "Careful now Marie, careful." They lifted something heavy out of the casket that had held the object for what must be many centuries. They were staring at a huge candelabra, a candelabra with seven arms.

Bérenger smiled and realised he could now build his Tower of Magdala, the tower he would dedicate to the Magdalene and which would forever survey the Rennes landscape, landscape of the Visigothic kingdom of Razès, landscape of the Cathar heresy and the landscape which had witnessed his own modest heresy with Emma.

But how could he turn the amazing golden object into the cash he needed to finance the works? This was the question which exercised his mind for many months. Every now and then he and Marie would take a candle late at night and set the great candelabra up in the darkest small room of the villa and, putting the largest candles they had been able to acquire in the seven holders, they would light the magnificent thing until the shadows cast a giant portrait of itself on the walls. One night they were both deeply affected by this action and the priest fell on his knees, followed quickly by the rustle of skirts as Marie knelt beside him. The priest offered up a prayer to the Lord thanking him for allowing him, Bérenger Saunière, to discover this treasure. And now he knew what he must do. He must melt the thing down, sell the gold and build his Tour Magdala.

And he must bury his love too. He would bury his love for Emma and rededicate new constructions to his love for Mary Magdalene. Some weeks later he painted the little relief sculpture under his new altar himself and Mary Magdalene in glowing yellow and blue sat serenely with the symbol of treasure at her feet. The treasure of King Solomon? The treasure of Love?

Antoine Cordier was enjoying working as the bell ringer partly because it gave him the excuse to visit Esperaza where he was sent by the priest to negotiate with the owner of the metal foundry for the price of casting a new bell for the church. Apart from his hobby of making little wooden figures of animals and saints Antoine had one abiding interest, pretty young women. He kept the latter interest secret from the priest but the little wooden figures enchanted the priest. He asked Antoine to bring some of his wooden figures to show him.

The priest particularly liked his carving in cedar wood of Mary and Jesus and asked him if he would be able to carve a Mary Magdalene. Antoine looked thoughtful.

"Was she the one that washed Our Lord's feet with ointment?"

The priest gave Antoine a five minute discourse on the Magdalene, without of course referring to the aspects of her life which had come to his knowledge recently. "Mary Magdalene landed at Saintes Maries de la Mer after the Crucifixion when she arrived in a boat from Egypt with Saintes Mary Jacob and Mary Salomé," explained the priest.

"I have been there and seen a wonderful statue in the crypt, wonderful! All the candles, I shall never forget," enthused Antoine. "If only I could make my sculpture like that!"

Saunière was already thinking if he could support Antoine's hobby and encourage him, he might be a useful provider of figures for the Tour Magdala project which he had in mind. Unlike his father, Antoine was not short of words and accepted the commission with many interjections about the joys of wood carving, keeping the priest from his dinner and causing Marie to scold him for this dreadful offence.

There were always pretty girls around in the market in Esperaza. One in particular he had his eye on had her own stall selling fruit and vegetables. He got through his meeting with the foundry owner as quickly as possible so he could pursue more important matters. "Your peaches look lovely and ripe," he said to the girl. She blushed the colour of one of her peaches.

"Oui monsieur, they were picked this morning. My mother and I have an orchard and I know we have the finest fruit in the whole of Languedoc." So saying she lifted a peach from the stall, cut off a slice and handed it to him smiling flirtatiously. He savoured the peach and the smile. He knew he was off to a good start with this girl and, as the juice ran down his chin, was already dreaming of a kiss from her red lips.

In his workshop Antoine set to work to carve a small

statue. He loved the rasp of the knife against the wood as his fingers flew expertly, releasing the image that he knew was hidden inside. The image of a golden haired young beauty, a bit like one of the saints thought Antoine, but also very like the girl in the Esperaza market. Musing about the colour of her lips and her soft smile, the inspiration came to him. That's it, he thought as he carved a round peach and settled it in her hands. She's bound to know what this means, thought Antoine.

Antoine's next visit to Esperaza was on a mission for the priest who had sent him to Molveau the foundry owner. The priest had told him to be very careful with the object which had been wrapped in a capacious blanket. "Take care, Antoine, I am entrusting it to you as I would trust it to the Virgin herself." Antoine was amazed at how heavy the blanket was but set off on his horse and cart to the village at the foot of the mountain. At one point the horse slipped on the stony road, the cart rocked and Antoine had to grab wildly for the heavy package which was inexorably being dragged to the edge of the cart and, but for a quick lunge by the desperate Antoine, could well have tumbled over the edge and crashed to the bottom of the mountain.

"Well that would have done for my chances of going to Esperaza and seeing that girl," he thought.

Antoine knew of Molveau from a previous visit the priest had sent him on. Molveau was a man who had himself been affected by his trade. Constantly in the heat of the foundry, even in the sizzling temperature of a Languedoc August, he was always drenched in sweat glistening on his torso and dripping in rivulets along the veins of his huge muscled biceps. His luxurious black moustache seemed to wave at him as Antoine approached.

"Ah little Antoine, what does the priest want now?" Antoine didn't care for the description but certainly acknowledged its accuracy in relation to the Samson-like Molveau.

"Monsieur, the priest wants you to melt down this thing." Antoine unfurled the old blanket and the massive Menorah clanged on to the stone floor. Antoine and Molveau stared at the huge object. "It's an old candelabra that belongs to the church," stuttered Antoine. "The priest has plenty of old candlesticks and he doesn't need another...but he needs the gold to manufacture a new altarpiece and to pay for his building repair works," continued Antoine as he, with Molveau, looked in amazement at the golden artefact at their feet.

"Mon dieu, that is some candlestick!"

As soon as he had left Molveau pondering on the candelabra, Antoine raced round to the market and looked anxiously around. There she is! Serving a fat lady from Couiza with a bunch of grapes. He caught her eye and saw a rosy glow suffuse her cheek. Waiting for his moment, he approached and took from his pocket the small statue and handed it to her.

"Oh," she looked at it surprised "C'est moi!"

"Do you like it?" asked Antoine. She smiled and nodded

and tucked it into her apron with an affectionate pat.

"I'm helping with the vendange. They will be starting it in a couple of weeks in the vineyard near St Paul de Fenouillet. Like to come?" Antoine felt he was risking everything with this bold suggestion. Young girls didn't offer to accompany young men they didn't know and away from their local neighbourhood, but Antoine had crafted his invitation well. The grape harvesting wouldn't be a very threatening place to be alone with a man as there would be many others there too.

"I get time off next week so if it's happening then I would like to go," she answered shyly.

The vendange was hard work, picking and cutting the juicy globes from their vines and bending over in the hot Languedoc sun. Even when Eloise cut her finger when the knife slipped, a little blood and a kissing of fingers and they were both smiling again. Youth and the excitement of being together made light of everything. While others, older in limb, cursed the heat, the young couple laughed and filled their baskets with mounds of juicy black grapes.

At the end of the last day of the vendange the vineyard owner brought kegs of wine for everyone. Most of the workers happily took a swig and went off home carrying their kegs and looking forward to an evening of drunken pleasure. Antoine and Eloise suddenly found themselves alone in the little vineyard hut where the workers kept their things during the day. As the clouds hovered over the Pyrénées the torrential rain was announced by a thunderous crack in the heavens. Sudden storms were not unusual here. The rain beat furiously on the tiled roof.

"We are stranded Eloise," whispered Antoine into the girl's ear with mock fear in his voice. She withdrew, a little panic seizing her.

"Maybe not for long, we might be able to run for it soon."

"Meanwhile let's have some of this wine we have worked so hard for," said Antoine as he proffered the keg to Eloise's lips and she gulped some down. The red liquid raced through her veins and she suddenly didn't feel like running through the rain. When Antoine kissed her she felt herself melting, her heart racing and soon she was lying on the straw palette on the floor, and there was Antoine's hand pushing up her skirt. Eloise did not even want to say, "Non."

Chapter 9

Wild Boar Hunt 1895

Molveau trudged up the hill early one morning with the intention of testing out with the priest his suspicion that there was more to this candelabra than met the eye.

"What do you mean Molveau? Do you imagine I sent Antoine to lie to you?"

"Non, non Monsignor, it's just that you may have made a mistake. You see I am wondering if this candelabra may even be a lost treasure. You must have heard rumours that the Visigoths brought treasure back from Rome after they sacked the city and may have buried it here in Razès. You see Monsignor, this candelabra could even be the Menorah, the lost treasure of the Temple of Solomon!"

"Vraiment! Molveau you can't really believe such a fairy tale," answered the priest, while marvelling at the perspicacity of the foundry owner. How does he know so much? Where did he get his knowledge of history from? How has he stumbled on the truth? He would have to deal carefully with him and, while not admitting to anything, keep him on his side. The priest invited the foundry owner to take a seat and poured a little libation of the golden liquid, Muscat de Rivesaltes. After several little libations there was a kind of understanding developing. Without exactly spelling it out

Molveau had managed to extract from the priest a share of the proceeds, in exchange for his silence, after he had melted down the gold candelabra.

Molveau walked down the hill with a light step, congratulating himself on outwitting the priest and getting a nice pile of gold for himself. Enough to buy himself a new farm and cultivate vines, to buy a mistress...maybe that delicious little Annette in Limoux. He licked his lips at the thought of her.

Saunière waited for Molveau to return with the news that the gold was ready. A month went by and he had heard nothing. Why was Molveau dragging his feet when there was such a big gain for him too? Molveau, at first elated and enthusiastic, had begun to have misgivings. He wondered if the candelabra were really genuine and wondered who he could get to verify its worth before undertaking the melting. And then there was a certain misgiving about melting the thing down at all. If it really was the Treasure of Solomon would it not be a sinful act to remove it from the world forever? Several times Molveau wandered over to his foundry in the evening to look at the candelabra. Every time as he prepared to do the deed he began to feel the doubts and sat staring at the candelabra for hours while he swigged from a bottle of red Fitou wine. Every time he ended up helplessly drunk and had to grope his way back to his house clinging onto the walls as he staggered back to a wife, who was angry with her husband's nocturnal outings and his inebriated return.

Saunière sent messages via Antoine and always got the same answer. M. Molveau was very busy with many important contracts but he would do it next month. The priest nevertheless continued from month to month to believe in the next month.

After several of his drinking episodes, Molveau decided he needed to take his mind off the candelabra, its promise of wealth or damnation. I'll get around to it next month he would promise himself. One evening as he mused, drinking and staring at the candelabra, he thought I don't have to wait for gold to go on a boar hunt though, thinking of his favourite pastime when he always felt his full masculine vigour, levelling the rifle at the boar, feeling himself bursting with energy and bonhomie. It would be a great way of having some fun. There was a hunt he could join next week. I'll ask that little Antoine to carry my provisions for me.

Antoine was polishing the gilt and dusting the plaster statues when he made up his mind to tell the priest.

"Monsignor can I have confession?"

"Why Antoine, I'm sure it's not that serious. Why don't you tell me what it is and then I'll decide whether you need confession."

"I lay with a girl from Esperaza and now she has a child. The baby is being looked after by a wet nurse which Eloise's mother found so that people in the village don't know that Eloise has had a baby. And that's not all, Monsignor, after I did the thing with Eloise I liked it so much I found other girls who would do it with me and now I don't know if the

Lord is angry with me," stuttered an embarrassed Antoine.

"Well Antoine, it looks like you might need confession after all but you must stop this sinful behaviour, marry Eloise and be a proper husband and father, then I'm sure Our Lord will forgive you."

"Oh, and something else, Father, M. Molveau has not done our job yet and he is going on a boar hunt tomorrow, but he has promised to do it definitely after the boar hunt." At this Saunière's optimism returned and he felt a tremor of excitement run through him and quickly forgot about Antoine's little misdemeanours, seeing him as a very trustworthy helpmate in his project. Yes, his good qualities certainly outweigh his bad thought the priest.

Antoine trudged, a bit reluctantly, behind Molveau loaded up with bags and a gun. He was still remembering Eloise and her soft body, her lips. "Come on Antoine, stop dreaming and give me the gun." Antoine quickly caught up and handed the impatient Molveau the weapon. The hunt was after a couple of big boars they had heard snorting amongst the vines. Antoine had never been on a boar hunt before and was feeling a bit nervous at the prospect of meeting one of these big beasts face to face. He picked up a large stone and cradled it in his hands. It would come in handy if one of them charged at him. At that moment a thunder of hoofs, a cloud of dust and the crack of a shot. But the boar kept coming. Antoine took aim with the stone and threw it with all his strength. The boar skidded to a halt and fell thunderously to the ground. Antoine had heard another shot too and wondered if it were his stone or Molveau's bullet that had got the boar. It was M. Dubois, the shopkeeper's gun and on the ground next to the boar lay an unfortunate Molveau, shot by his friend and now never to enjoy the fruits of the candelabra's gold.

A bedraggled and stuttering Antoine burst into the church looking for the priest.

"Terrible news! I went on the boar hunt and he was shot. Horrible it was, the blood, his matted hair where the blood had trickled out of his head, you would not have believed it. Terrible, terrible..."

"Calm down Antoine, if you go on a boar hunt you must expect to see a boar shot. You will smile well enough when it ends up on your plate as a tasty boar stew I'm sure."

"No, no, no, not the boar, well yes the boar too, but I think I killed that with a stone."

"Antoine are you lying to me, a stone never killed a boar and you are not a very good shot."

"I am now, I got him on the snout and it bounced up between his eyes and he fell over just like huge sack of potatoes. But it's M.Molveau."

"M.Molveau? What's M.Molveau, Antoine?"

"He's dead."

"Dead? No Antoine, I saw him only yesterday."

"That's as maybe but he's dead now. Dead as ...as...as you would be, begging your pardon, if a bullet was to hit you in the head. Or me sir. No, he's gone sir. It was an accident. M. Dubois was trying to get the boar but he tripped as he pressed the trigger. At least that's what he's saying now. Otherwise he murdered him!"

The priest reflected on this strange turn of events, and while saying a silent blessing for Molveau's soul, he thought that now his secret was safe and the true origin of the candelabra and the gold would never be known to anyone else. I will muse upon this great event for our village, for certainly there will be questions asked.

"Doubtless his wife will be making the arrangements for her husband's funeral with me soon, Antoine. Meanwhile go home and get some rest."

A few weeks after Molveau had been put to rest and the local Inspector of Police had interviewed M. Dubois and Antoine, the village calmed down and Antoine, while wondering why the accident had happened, began to apply himself to another idea. He would carve a wonderful statue of the Magdalene for the priest. He knew the priest had a plan to rededicate the church to Mary Magdalene and this would be a gift for him, to thank him for looking after his soul, and yes he would give up those two other girls in Esperaza, even if they are so pretty and in love with him. They will be mad with him but he has decided to marry Eloise and settle down. The statue would be his promise to live a proper life.

Saunière held the little carving of the Magdalene in his hand. "It is beautiful Antoine." He was filled with awe as he gazed into the Magdalene's eyes. Yes, Antoine was a strange one indeed, a real artist, he had endowed the little statue with a soul and created a sacred object. The priest felt the presence of the Magdalene as he had known it in the séance at Emma's salon in Paris. Now he had an inspiration, a divine command? To place the little statue under the foundations of the Tour Magdala. The buried Magdalene and the altar image would, he was sure, endow his church with the powerful Spirit of the Magdalene and when he had built his Tour Magdala, make it the premier site in all of France dedicated to her. The Tower would survey the whole plain of the Razès and send its holy energy to radiate out over the very landscape where Debussy had been so inspired. The energy would bless the magical landscape of Languedoc, would heal the old Cathar wounds, would be so magnetic that many new pilgrims would be attracted to Rennes-le-Château in the coming years well into the unforeseen future.

Saunière forgot in his ecstasy that the melting down of the candelabra would not now happen and he wouldn't have the gold he needed to accomplish his visionary plan. He must see Emma and ask her help from her wealthy friends. Seized with this idea he threw everything in confusion with Marie, packing a bag and telling her he was going to Paris. She felt a pain in the region of her heart and clutched her bosom in fear. As the pain passed she knew it was jealousy striking at her innermost being. She suspected him of going to meet his lover in that wicked city. He would come back more crazy than ever and there would be no peace for her in Rennes.

Chapter 10

Return to Paris 1895

As Saunière stepped onto the platform at the Gare d'Orsay he was filled with foreboding. What if she didn't want to see him, what if she had another lover and even now....no he couldn't bear it. He hailed a hansom cab to his lodgings in rue Daunou and almost missed the delightful scenes from the carriage window as all Paris seemed to pass him by and once again he was able to savour the throbbing vitality of that magnificent city, see the new boulevards built by the energetic Baron Haussmann under Napoleon III, and wonder at the realisation that in the 1860s the whole of Paris must have been some gigantic building site – and now what a wonder had been created. The carriage clattered over the cobbles as it wheeled a little recklessly around the great Place de l'Opéra and he saw again, but in daylight this time, Charles Garnier's ornate palace with its statues of the great musicians, Bach, Mozart, Beethoven and, above all, topped by the golden statues of Orpheus plucking his lyre on each of the two great turrets of the opera house. Yes, grandiose, that's the word. How magnificent Paris is, thought Saunière, smiling delightedly to himself.

Once in his small lodgings he asked for the concierge to come and see him. She was a bony little woman who reminded him rather of the ladies who were said to sit knitting around Mme Guillotine. "Madame, would you arrange to send this note for me. It must get there this afternoon."

"I'll send my boy, sir," she said taking the note from his hand and glancing at the address. She recognised it as one of the posh addresses in Paris so this man must know some wealthy people she thought.

"Tell your boy to wait for an answer."

"Yes sir," she replied and pocketed the note in her grubby overall. The reply took two days to come and Saunière had fretted in his lodgings while taking the occasional saunter to see the splendours of his now beloved Paris. The hill of Montmartre, the surprising vineyard, the street girls, the flower sellers, the carriages, the beautiful ladies and their finely turned out male companions in the Parc, all this offered him substitutes for seeing his Emma, but rather like a man being fed on caviar when he really fancies a hearty steak, he felt uneasy and wondered if his journey was in vain?

Now holding the scented envelope in his hand he trembled.

Dearest

How good to know you have business in Paris. Please come to visit me at 8 o'clock this evening. I will await you.

Emma

He pressed the envelope to his lips inhaling its intoxicating scent. Emma! Emma! Emma!

Reaching the steps of her mansion he hesitated. The footman let him in. Did he detect an attempt to hide a smirk? This time the house was empty and instead of being overawed by the people he had time to take in the paintings on the curving staircase. There was one of Leda and the Swan, another of Troilus and Cressida and a scene from Romeo and Juliet. So Emma was a patron of the arts – and of passion? The large door swung open under the touch of the white gloved hand on the door handle, followed by a discreet retiring step backwards as it became obvious that he should enter on his own. An alluring scent assailed his nostrils as he suddenly found himself alone in the grand suite. "Bérenger," a whispered voice came from an inner sanctum and he found himself following it to a door which stood slightly ajar. As he pushed it gently he saw her, reclining in a diaphanous negligée on a silk covered grand lit. "Viens ici, mon chéri." He needed no further encouragement. His love was back!

Some hours later she pulled on a bell rope to call the footman to bring them champagne. Bérenger listened excited by the sound of the pop of the cork as it released the bubbles and he heard the trickle of the liquid as the footman poured two glasses and whispered "Madame" in an intonation which clearly stated he had done his duties and would now depart, leaving the lovers to their private joys. Emma leapt out of bed trailing the negligée which had slipped revealing her breasts.

She returned bearing the two glasses.

"As I sip this marvellous champagne I think of the champagne we drink in Rennes...Blanquette de Limoux. You know the monks at the Abbaye St Hilaire, which is just a short way away from Rennes invented it before champagne was invented. The monk who had come up with his magic liquid told his fellow monks that the drink had stars in it. And ..."

"Stop!" She put a finger on his lips. "And now Monsignor priest tell me what has really brought you to Paris apart from seeing me?"

He told the story of the discovered treasure of the candelabra of the Temple of Solomon and of the Magdalene statue which had inspired him and his need for money now that there was to be no melting down of the gold owing to the sad death of M. Molveau. She listened attentively and, looking upwards at the cherubs painted on her ceiling, said, "I think I may be able to help, but forget your country champagne, this is Dom Perignon, the real thing!" She kissed him and then the stars were indeed in the champagne.

One of Emma's aristocratic friends was the Archduke Johann Salvator, the nephew of the Emperor Franz Josef of Austria. She had hinted to him about the Magdalene secret and he would be more than willing to listen to anything related to this mystery. Bérenger was getting out of his depth now but a meeting was nevertheless arranged with Johann who was living in Paris at the Hotel George V this season. Emma told the priest not to be nervous of meeting Johann:

"He is the brother of Crown Prince Rudolf, he is très sympathique, and is a very interesting man. He is a man who has secrets. He is in love with a maid of honour at the Hapsburg court. She has completely enchanted him and he is determined to marry her but he is concealing it from his mother who would be totally horrified. He carries around Milli's likeness in a miniature portrait concealed in his ring."

Bérenger found himself surprisingly at ease with the Archduke, a very personable and handsome young man with a dashing appearance. Emma and he were obviously on very close terms; she addressed him as "Johann liebling." The rough priest appealed to Johann as the kind of man he got on with despite the difference in rank. The priest was direct and rather rigid in bearing like himself but had an uncanny whiff of enigma about him, typical of Emma's séance friends. On hearing the candelabra story his interest lit up like the candles themselves did when he first lit them in Rennes, thought Bérenger. But his true interest was in hearing more about Mary Magdalene's appearance and apparent involvement in the priest's plans. Johann was never sure of his beliefs outside the doctrines of his Catholic faith but his sense of curiosity compelled him not to miss a chance to at least investigate the stranger realms. After a while he interrupted Emma's excited championing of Bérenger's need for money to follow the Magdalene's instructions to build a tower dedicated to her in Rennes-le-Château.

"On a visit to Rome last year I explored the ruins of the Roman Forum and came across the Titus Arch. There above my head I saw the great Menorah carved into the monument. There and then I longed to find this lost treasure. That you, Monsignor, have found it causes me great joy and amazement. I will provide you with the money you need to complete the Magdalene's Tower and only ask that you let me take the candelabra back to my castle in Austria."

Bérenger was so excited, he clapped the surprised Archduke on the shoulder as he thanked him with a fervour that left the Austrian annoyed and amused at the same time. He clicked his heels and took his leave. "Farewell, M. Saunière you will receive word from my courier."

Tour Magdala, Rennes-le-Château

Chapter 11

The Tour Magdala 1895 - 1900

A few months later in Rennes-le-Château, the elderly Gelis, the priest of nearby Rennes-le-Bain arrived on Saunière's doorstep. The two priests went into a private room and Marie, listening at the door as was her habit, heard talk of the tower and Austria and money but couldn't make a lot of sense of it. Gelis had been selected as courier by Johann because he was known to Austrian contacts and had been invited to Austria by Johann for reasons unconnected with his real motive, to use him as a cash conduit to Saunière.

Bérenger hurried down the hill to Couiza and found M. Caminade, the architect, in his office. Bursting in, red faced, he waved a piece of paper with a rough sketch of a tower which he had drawn and blurted out triumphantly, "Caminade, I want you to design this tower." Caminade had been privy to Bérenger's dream of building a tower but never thought he'd ever be able to do it. Where would a poor parish priest get the money from? Well, it seems as if the money has come from somewhere, it's not for me to question where from, he thought.

When the Tour Magdala was finally built Bérenger crept in at night and buried the statue of the Magdalene under a geometric patterned tile; the tile featured an eight pointed star like the others on the floor but was very slightly different in the tone colour of the background, hardly noticeable but enough for Bérenger to remember under which tile lay the Secret. Bérenger's passion for Emma was confused with his adoration of the Magdalene. He felt the pain of leaving Emma in Paris and the torture of imagining her with other lovers, with his profound joy at being closer to the Magdalene in his own Rennes-le-Château. Bérenger wistfully realised that the dedication of the tower to the Magdalene was also a dedication to his temporal love for Emma.

After praying to the Magdalene that night Bérenger picked up his diary and wrote. "Today I sanctified my love for Emma and my adoration of the Magdalene in my own sacred place. I see my love for Emma fusing with that of the Magdalene, the Black Madonna, and see that the Magdalene is the true face of the Sacred Feminine which will come to be revered again in the world as in the ancient times when she was worshipped through the ritual of Hieros Gamos. The arcadian joys of love touch my heart and my soul – Et in Arcadia Ego."

Musing on these thoughts on one of his wanderings alone into the countryside, Bérenger once again found himself in front of the tomb near Arques which was so reminiscent of the Poussin painting he had bought a print of on his visit to the Louvre. The painting Et in Arcadia Ego seemed to him to be of this very tomb with the landscape of Rennes in the background. Debussy had told him that Poussin was one of the past Grand Masters of the Prieuré de Sion so it was not surprising that he would leave clues to the Secret in his work. Bérenger had also discovered on his visit to St Sulpice in Paris, that the Paris Meridian runs from this imposing church, second only to Notre Dame, and passes through Arques, Rennes le Bain and Bugarach on its way to Villefranche de Conflent where the very skull of St Sulpice is housed. So, thought Saunière, the Paris Meridian points to this place as the perfect place to hide the Secret and to portray it in painting. And rounds it off neatly by pointing to the significance of St Sulpice at both ends of France!

Salvador Dalí in Collioure

Chapter 12

Cadaques Spain 1930

Salvador was swimming amongst the dolphins when Gala shouted across the water, "Your new model has arrived!" He swam languorously to the shore of the little cove of Port Lligat, shook himself as he got out of the water into the hot sunshine beating down, felt the heat already drying up the beads of sea from his athletic body. Looking up he saw a beautiful young woman standing with Gala on the steps of the house he and his wife had created together as a private and unique space on this remote, glorious bay of the Catalan coast. The poet Paul Eluard had visited the previous summer with his wife Gala. Gala and Salvador had instantly been attracted to each other and Gala knew that before the summer was over she would not go back to Paris with Paul. Well, the central tenet of Surrealism was free love so Paul ought to get over his jealousy.

"Monsieur Dalí, je m'appelle Françoise." She extended a small white hand to Salvador, a formality that he wasn't expecting. He took her hand in his and raised it to his lips. "Bienvenue Mademoiselle à Port Lligat. I was not expecting a French girl. Where are you from?" "Over the border in Languedoc, Monsieur, the town of Esperaza."

Getting to know Françoise over the next few weeks of the

modelling contract proved a delightful surprise for the Spanish painter. Not only an opportunity to practise his French but also an opportunity to enjoy her delightful wit and fund of stories from her region of France. He adored her astonishingly beautiful figure as he drew her, enjoying the curves as they were formed by his pencil. She found him to be the strangest man she had ever encountered, wild and erratic, funny even, certainly a little crazy and very attractive. His wife Gala watched like a hawk, so she was aware that her flirting with him was dangerous.

That he was a magnet for other artists of the avant garde became quickly apparent. Even in this remote place they were visited by people who descended on the villa. Françoise met other painters, Juan Gris, Picasso, Picabia and writers from Paris. Even René Magritte, the strange Belgian who painted pictures of bowler hats and umbrellas, visited. Françoise was enchanted, watching him with his easel on the beach and instead of dolphins there was a tuba and a chair appearing from under his brush on his canvas. She was beginning to get some idea of what surrealism was and she was clever enough to see this was a special world full of revolutionary ideas and exciting people. She wanted to be a part of it. It was a passport to an exciting new Bohemian life which would enable her to leave her lovely but boring Languedoc village for the pleasures of Paris and the excitement of being admired by great artists. This surreal stuff was really strange but no stranger, she mused, than the story of Rennes-le-Château. And all of them wanted to paint her if she ever came to Paris. Although she suspected their enthusiasm to paint her masked a hope or even expectation that they could get her into their bed. Well, she wouldn't mind too much, she could see this surrealism was very much about eroticism which would hardly leave untouched the desires of these heroic artists. She was beginning to see herself as the Muse of Surrealism much as Renoir's girls were his Muses.

Dalí had done many sketches of her during the first month. Then one beautiful morning he began to lay out his oil paints in the little white room which overlooked the bay and prepared an enormous canvas.

"Françoise! Come here and take your clothes off. I have an idea for a painting which will make you famous. Lie down on the sofa. I will paint you as a fish."

She smiled, knowing that with Salvador there was no chance of being painted just as a woman. As she slowly removed her clothes he felt aroused by her beauty. He painted frantically, shouting at her now and again to keep still, to move, to change position. He was in a trance as the canvas filled with his erotically charged surreal vision. Ten hours later, with only a brief break, he had completed his masterpiece. He flung the brush down, knocked over a pot of paint as he approached her. "Come and look my dear." He took her hand and led her to the canvas.

She stood there, her mind spinning as she took in the extraordinary scene on the canvas. She had never seen anything like this in her life. Strange as it was she instantly knew it was the work of a genius.

"Look Françoise, see this," he indicated the large head on its side... "his immense nose reclining on the onyx floor, his enormous eyelids closed, his brow frightfully furrowed with wrinkles..."

But she was looking for herself, her image, it was there in the convoluted, wild shapes that his inspired imagination had transformed it to. He has made me into a woman from his dream world and now I am the Muse for Dalí too, she thought, from now on it won't be just Gala who is his muse it will be me! I, Françoise, will inspire this mad genius's exciting surrealist vision. She had been waiting for another moment too. Sensing his rising passion as he looked at her, waiting for her reaction. "It is..." she paused, "...unusual!" Her dark eyes met his. "Now, Maître, do whatever you want," she whispered encouragingly.... intuitively sensing what he wanted, what he needed.

As they lay in each other's arms she said, "I have a title for your painting."

"What is that?"

She smiled and whispered in his ear, "The Great Masturbator."

Dalí stroked his formidable moustache. "Et toi, Françoise, tu est digne de Maître!"

Dalí and Françoise shared no more close encounters. Dalí's guilt to his Saviour, his Muse Gala, was too strong to permit more sexuality but they shared a different kind of intimacy. Françoise was a great storyteller and he was a great fantasist so they enjoyed, while painting, talking and weaving elegant stories and surrealist visions which fed Salvador's own poetry. While drawing Françoise one day he wrote a poem inspired by The Great Masturbator.

All the love and all the ecstasy
of the Great Masturbator
resided
in the cruel ornaments of false gold
covering his delicate and soft temples
imitating
the shape of an imperial crown
whose fine leaves of bronze acanthus
reached as far
as his rosy and beardless cheeks
and extended their hard fibres
until they dissolved
in the clear alabaster of his neck

Françoise told him more about her life and one day startled Dalí with a tale from her mother's life. "Ma mère, Eloise, she and my father, Antoine, were close to learning about a fabulous secret, the truth about a treasure which Abbé Saunière had discovered in the little village of Rennes-le-Château...you have heard the story perhaps Maître?"

She recounted the whole thing as she had heard it from her mother's lips. Dalí was intrigued, fascinated, and immediately decided to go to Rennes-le-Château himself and confirm the truth of her story. After all, she might be a

Model of Salvador Dalí in Cadaques

fantasist too and may have embroidered this tale of treasure and religious mystery involving Our Lord and Mary Magdalene.

Salvador stepped off the train from Figueras. He had arrived in Perpignan. Leaving Perpignan station Dalí felt a curious sensation throughout his body and shivered in the heat. A bright light appeared above him. Within stood the Archangel Michael with flaming sword. The vision swirled around, shattering his composure and opening up his very soul to a message which only the great Dalí could hear. He was in ecstasy now as the enchanted angel told him, "This is the Centre of the Universe!"

"Are you alright sir?" A hand gripped his elbow and he welcomed its steadying influence. He saw the young railwayman looking concerned. "I never felt better," he exclaimed exultantly. "Did you know that you work in the Centre of the Universe?" The porter looked really worried now as he reluctantly let go of the distinguished man's arm. The railwayman sauntered back into the station glad to get away from the stranger.

His whole being on fire with the angelic encounter Dalí was indeed ready to explore the mystery of Rennes-le-Château. His chauffeur, Mario, was waiting for him. After a bumpy car ride in his Hispano Suiza, the car laboured up the perilous mountain track to the village perched on the summit like a hidden kingdom.

As he climbed out of the magnificent automobile Salvador noticed that the Hispano Suiza badge had the very same wings worn by the Archangel Michael. Entering the strange porch of the church Dalí encountered a devilish statue of Asmodeus who leered at him evilly, forcing him back on his heels to see above the horrible image the four angels of benediction giving the sign of the cross. In His name we shall conquer. Somewhat reassured Dalí continued into the Church.

At the altar stood a painting of Mary Magdalene. Above the painting she appeared in glorious light welcoming him forward. "Si Senor Dalí you have come to the church at the centre of the universe for that is what this place really is. The truth was buried here by the Cathars and will now be revealed to you, the only worthy pilgrim who understands how the world of the unconscious realms meet with the every day to create magic and miracles. The miracle here truly is the hidden secret discovered by the Abbé Saunière that Jesus and I were married and performed the sacred rite of Hieros Gamos. A ritual to transform the pain of the crucifixion into love and ignored by the later Church. Yes, there is a Bloodline and it is blessed.

"As for material treasure there is that too buried under this church by the Cathars who escaped from Montsegur. Now Senor go back to Cadaques and take this secret with you. Perhaps you will find a way to put it in one of your paintings or even sculptures. Remember Hannibal crossed the Pyrenees here with his elephants so perhaps that would be an idea for you." Dalí crossed himself on his knees before the holy vision of Mary Magdalene. He stumbled and dropped his wallet as he tried to get up. Picking up the notes that had fallen on the floor he gathered his wits and his possessions together and left the church in a daze of excitement. "Mario, get me a drink and we're going home."

Dalí returned from Rennes and on his first portrait session with Françoise burst out with excitement. "I have conceived an extraordinary idea, a surreal journey through time in which chance would play a significant part. Imagine a trail studded with enigmatic clues – a truly surreal experience for the mind! Only matched by my vision for the Teatro Dalí where my art will one day create a museum where the building itself will be the surrealist box containing my jewels, my visions."

Seizing Françoise by the arm he guided her to the window. "Look, my dear, this you think is my world but I have discovered through you a new world, a world which is not bounded by this bay, or by the borders of Spain but is a surreal, historic, paranoiac region which unites the fate of the Cathars, the Mystery of Rennes-le-Château and the blessed Mary Magdalene with the surreal vision of Dalí! And the centre of this world is not here in Cadaques but in Perpignan!"

"In Perpignan?"

"Oui, Françoise, listen to me, it was there at the railway station that I, Dalí, was given the Truth! As I arrived at the Gare de Perpignan suddenly everything appeared to me with the clarity of light...I found myself in front of the Centre of the Universe. What does this mean, I wondered and then after I had wrestled with this problem I realised that if you describe a circle around Perpignan radiating north, south, west and east it captures in its circle Montségur, where the Cathars were burnt, Rennes-le-Château where the treasure and the mystery of Mary Magdalene were buried, Minerve where Simon de Montfort burnt Cathars and here, yes here where Dalí lives and has been pursuing his visions dragged from his unconscious dreams. Yes, Perpignan is the centre of this universe but it is also a mini universe which is of great importance to a new understanding of spirituality and the unseen worlds. And I, Salvador Dalí, have been given this knowledge by the Divine Source because my work is so important in uniting the spiritual and the erotic and the nature of man.

"And more, Françoise, everything I have said unites the story of the buried treasure, which the Cathars had been the custodians of, and had buried in Rennes, with the Secret of Mary Magdalene and Jesus which had been also held by the Cathars, and was the reason their religion was wiped out. I have been chosen to immortalise the Secret and to carry it forward as I am now the custodian. Because hidden meanings are only capable of interpretation by the true seeker, I have been chosen to hide the meanings within my work and ideas. In this way I will lay the trail for a True Seeker to find the Secret and, when the time is ripe, reveal it to the world."

Chapter 13

Languedoc 1244

Pierre knew what would happen to the others. The flames. He had always had a horror of fire so if he had to risk his life clambering down this almost perpendicular side of Montségur that was better than burning. Pierre was a skilled climber. His father Amaury, had taken him with him on his travels to the scattered villages of the Ariège from his sixth birthday. They had encountered many hills and difficult terrain for a little boy's legs but Pierre soon found himself able to deal with all sorts of difficulties which would have been impossible for other children. Once, when his father had been returning from Mirepoix where he had been selling his leather baskets and the cloaks that his wife made, they had been suddenly engulfed in a fierce blizzard and had to take shelter in a cave until the next day. The climb up to the cave with the snow stinging his face, tears falling down his cheeks, was coming back to him now as he struggled with every foothold. He remembered his father's strong hand holding his and giving him strength. He felt that hand in his as he slipped and stumbled downwards and then letting go as his feet landed on firm ground.

Authie had been given instructions by Esclarmonde where to take the treasure. First to Château Usson to join the other half of the Cathar treasure which had been smuggled out of Montségur some months ago, stored in a well hidden cave in the hills beyond Usson. They were to go to Count Raymonde, the Lord of Usson, a Cathar sympathiser, and to take the two parts of the treasure to another more secure hiding place where it could remain until there was a possibility of refounding a Cathar community. If this wasn't possible in the near future, the Cathar teachings spoke of a time in 750 years when Catharism would return to the Languedoc. The power within the treasure was said to be great and would in the future be able to bring peace and harmony to the world.

The Count received the three Cathars with enthusiasm but with a sad demeanour.

"My friends," he said, "the fate of your companions was indeed dreadful. They refused to convert and went singing into the flames. Even the soldiers you knew who were not Cathars converted at the last minute and joined them devotedly. My spies among the besiegers tell me their screams were terrible but they all entered the flames voluntarily."

Pierre sobbed at the thought of the lovely Esclarmonde being consumed by the fire. The others mourned their loved ones but all three knew that they had been released from the 'tunics' of their bodies and were now pure Soul and Spirit as was the true end of all Cathar believers.

Beyond their despair was the momentous burden of responsibility that rested on them. To save the Cathar treasure and to ensure its safety before any soldiers could catch up with them. The Count provided a guide to the cave which would otherwise have been impossible to find. Etienne led them up into the mountainous area behind Usson and Axat.

"What is that?" exclaimed Authie.

A large bird flapped its wings over their heads, its claws threatening to rip off their hair, as they dived to the ground.

"The Sentinel Eagle!" shouted Etienne. "It guards the treasure and won't let anyone near the cave."

At this explanation the bird settled itself at the mouth of the cave, glaring threateningly at the advancing men.
Pierre approached slowly but quickly leapt back as the eagle emitted a terrifying scream.

"How do we get past it?" whispered Pierre.

"Show it the treasure that Esclarmonde gave you in Montségur," suggested Etienne.

Pierre scrabbled in the leather bag and pulled out the gold brooch inscribed with the initials MM. He remembered the moment when Esclarmonde had given it him with such reverence.

"This is the most precious jewel in the world, take it and guard it," she had said.

He realised now he had loved her or maybe worshipped her from afar. Saying a quick prayer for Esclarmonde's soul, he gingerly walked ahead, the brooch glinting in the bright sunlight giving off a dazzling light. The eagle shuffled its feathers, made what Pierre could have sworn was a kind of bow and stepped aside. Pierre saw the Cathar cross first, hanging above a wooden box secured with a metal hoop.

After struggling down the mountain with the heavy chest, the Count provided them with a horse and cart and gave them careful instructions on where to lay the treasure to rest. In the Razès, the old Visigoth land where Solomon's treasure had been brought from Rome when Alaric, the Visigoth, sacked the Holy City.

Cathar Memorial

Chapter 14

Languedoc 1310

Guilhem Bélibaste stirred in the bed and flung his arm around the sleeping Raymonde. He had slept well. He felt more or less safe in Toroella. Fleeing the Inquisition had been difficult but he had finally completed the difficult journey over the Pyrénées from France and knew the Spanish would never turn him in to the French Inquisition. He clambered out of the big wooden bed and fell to his knees praising and thanking God for his safety now. "Blessed Jesus merci, merci, merci." Being a latecomer to Catharism he still found himself following some of the old forms of prayer, but he was a true and devoted follower of the Cathar faith. Very conscious of his humble origins as a shepherd in the Corbières, and still remorseful of the murder he had committed when he killed a peasant out of sheer anger 10 years ago, Guilhem was now one of the few Good Men who had survived the persecution of the Pope's Crusade against the remaining Cathars. Fifty years ago they had rooted out the survivors of the massacres of Montségur, Béziers and Minerve, those who had created their own secret, safe sanctuary in the village of Montaillou in the Ariège, living as Catholics but maintaining their Cathar beliefs in dualism. They knew with a conviction of revelation that their bodies were simply tunics which their God given souls were forced to live in on this earth until they could reclaim the Spirit on death through obtaining the consolamentum, the blessing ministered by one of the Parfaits, the Bon Hommes. Guilhem was himself a Parfait, a Good Man, but he was worried that he may be the only surviving one of his kind and, with his death, what would happen to the survivng Cathars seeking the absolution as the promised gateway to heaven and the life of the Spirit?

Raymonde stirred and purred, "Forget praying now and come back to bed." Guilhem looked at her, taking in the olive skin, the tousled red hair, the curve of her exposed breast.

"No! Raymonde, I have asked for guidance and I know now what to do. We feel safe in Spain but this is an illusion. People know that as a Parfait I am not allowed to live with a woman. And yet I cannot leave you my love." He went to her and seized her in his arms and as he covered her with kisses whispered in her ear, "You are my weakness...the weakness which will prevent me from ever taking the final consolamentum myself. You, my dear must marry."

Pushing him away and staring into his eyes Raymonde exclaimed, "Marry! But how is that possible? We cannot marry."

"Not to me my dear, but to Pierre Clergue. This way we will escape scrutiny and Pierre will know you are still my woman. He will probably enjoy you on the wedding night though."

Bélibaste had to secure their position and it wasn't difficult to persuade Pierre, always his loyal friend, but who long had a lustful eye for the beautiful Raymonde. The wedding was quickly arranged and to all the eyes of the onlookers it seemed that the couple were in love and in good spirits as they invited the throng to their wedding feast. The usually meagre table groaned with a pig's head, capons, quails and sweetmeats. The people indulged, welcoming this respite from their usual vegetarian diet only allowed at special feasts.

The next day Bélibaste felt unusually irritable. He could not stop his ears from the sounds from the room where Raymonde and Pierre were spending their wedding night. He felt unexpected pangs in his heart which, on examination, he recognised as jealousy, an emotion he had never felt before which now unfamiliarly tormented him. No use to say he had himself to blame. A vivid picture emerged in his mind of Raymonde, naked and passionately responding to Pierre's caresses throughout the night. Bélibaste, his head in his hands, tried to blot out the vision that came to him of white stallions snorting and pounding through the forest accompanied by the sounds of hunting horns. He moaned softly like a child in pain. Damn her! He tormented himself with the thought that she had entered into the arrangement a little too enthusiastically!

But now Bélibaste had other business to attend to. The strange visitor, Arnauld Sicre, had got into his system. Arnauld had appeared one day announcing himself as searching for the Cathars and describing himself as a French

Cathar. He had heard that he could find safety with fellow Cathars in Toroella. At first Bélibaste was suspicious of this lone Cathar but soon warmed to him when he showed him such respect and admiration. Arnauld was forever wanting to serve him with little tasks, helping with his carding business, even helping Raymonde with her household duties. This was unusual in a man but Arnauld was following the Cathar belief that men and women are equal and had found an original way of putting it into practical action.

Arnauld began to play on Bélibaste's dreams of France with talk of his wealthy aunt who, as a Cathar sympathiser, wanted to donate a large sum of money to help the formation of Cathar communities in safe havens such as the very one that Arnauld had now discovered that Guilhem was founding in Toroella. Guilhem spent many tortured nights worrying over the problem whether to take the journey over the mountains to France with Arnauld.

"Yes, we will go," he told Arnauld. "Get some things together and we leave tomorrow."

The journey was difficult, the mountains treacherous, the weather bad and Bélibaste's suspicions of Sicre growing. He decided to get him drunk and see if he could trip him up but the only result was Sicre seemed to be completely genuine. Although he was blubbing out all sorts of stuff, he never fell into any of Guilhem's traps that he had set, so he ended up, also a little drunk, flinging his arms around Arnauld and calling him "Brother".

Bélibaste gave thanks to God as his feet trod on French

soil again. They were on the road to Mirepoix where Sicre's aunt lived and would doubtless be relieved that her nephew had had such great success in locating the secret Cathar community in Spain.

The moment of relief was over very quickly as they approached the outskirts of Mirepoix. Bélibaste was suddenly thrown to the ground. Arnauld had grasped his arm, twisted it and flung him to the ground, calling out triumphantly, "Here he is!" Soldiers emerged from behind the trees, took hold of both men and bound them up.

They were imprisoned together in the same cell.

"Brother, why did you betray me?"

Sicre remained silent, nursing his arms to his chest and squatting in the corner of the cell. It wasn't long before he was questioned by the Tribunal who satisfied themselves that he was an informer and sent him off with his reward for entrapping Bélibaste.

Bélibaste, alone now, forced to face himself, his life and his Cathar faith, missed Raymonde, longed to feel her arms around him, her lips, and knew he would never see her again. Is this what Christ felt as he gazed down from the cross on the weeping Magdalene? He comforted himself with the thought of meeting again in the Spirit when they had both departed the 'tunics' of their bodies which they had been forced to wear on earth.

The Archbishop of Narbonne faced Bélibaste and in a fierce contest of wills attempted to find out what really motivated these heretical beliefs. The Archbishop came across a formidable opponent, an orator and a convinced heretic.

"If you persist in this heresy, Bélibaste, you know you will burn at the stake. Why not do the sensible thing and return to Mother Church. The flames are terrible, Bélibaste. Renounce your evil beliefs and you can go free."

Bélibaste felt the awful tug of life, the yearning for Raymonde, seeing the birds in the sky, treading the ground of Languedoc in the spring when the vines were beginning to sprout their green leaves. A simple word would regain all of this for him. His refusal meant facing the death he had always dreaded most since he had heard the tales of Montségur. He also knew that in death he could not even be certain of passing onto the spirit level as a Parfait Cathar as he had surrendered to his weakness for a woman, so he may have to face another incarnation. How many years ahead? Who could know?

Bélibaste was taken to the village of Villerouge Termenès in the Corbières, not so far from the other Cathar châteaux he had once spent time in with his friends, Quéribus, Aguilar. The interrogation by the Archbishop and the Inquisition did not shake his Cathar faith. He had the power within himself, of the knowledge of where the Cathar treasure was hidden, of the truth of the marriage of Jesus and Mary Magdalene, these secrets he would not divulge. He was dragged through the narrow cobblestoned streets to the Place where the pyre was waiting for him. What cruelty, he thought, as he reflected on Christ's message of love and the weird way His words are interpreted by his priests. What love is in the pyre that burns the Good Men, those who have proclaimed the truth of Christ to their followers? He as the last Perfect One, was to be exterminated by the Church. Proof enough that the Evil Satan had created the material world and that he now empowers his priests to solidify his rule, his misrule.

Bélibaste tasted the fear in his dry mouth as he prepared himself to give up his Spirit and enter the fire. As the pyre was lit he begged his God for courage and prayed. Something strange happened to him in his last moments and, although the pain was terrible, he felt himself uplifted, experiencing a sense of optimism and conviction. Recovering his voice he shouted out, "Seven hundred years Catharism will return and be a light for humanity!" As the choking smoke reached his lungs threatening to burst them he saw a vision of a beautiful new world emerging from pain and suffering to a new era of peace and love. "Love triumphs," and then, "Raymonde," he muttered to himself as the flames consumed the 'tunic' of this life.

The Archbishop smiled and whispered, "Excellent, the Last Cathar is dead."

L'Espace Dalí

Chapter 15

Paris 2004

Madeleine and Bernard took the No 68 bus from the top of the Rue d'Amsterdam. This was a great bus, the route surpassed that of almost any tour bus as it careered past the Moulin Rouge, and dropped them at the Opéra house designed by the flamboyant Charles Garnier as a 19th century temple of love and music.

"There's something about this opera house which evokes Saunière himself," whispered Madeleine as they ascended the fabulous marble staircase. "Look some of the marble is from Languedoc."

Bernard stared at the red and cream whirlpool effect of the balustrade and recalled the same thing he had seen in Languedoc. He remembered the legend that Emma Calvé had visited Saunière in Rennes-le-Château and the story that they had been lovers. This was where Emma had sung Carmen and had enchanted the priest Saunière. Sitting in their cherub-decked box, the scene provided a magical setting for the ecstasy of Tchaikowsky's romantic tragedy Eugene Onegin. Bernard felt the warmth of Madeleine's hand squeezing his as the soprano reached for the high C.

At the Café de la Paix after the opera they sat with a coffee and Pernod.

"It's Emma, she was his lover, I am sure of it. When watching Onegin tonight and the story of his admirer writing to Eugene to tell him she was in love with him and, at first, his refusal to believe it or take any real note of it, which leads to her despair and near suicide, I knew this was what had happened to Emma!"

"What, with Saunière? He was hardly a romantic character, a rather ordinary country parish priest," Bernard said.

"You are right, but don't you see that was why, it was Emma's flaw, she had had many romantic young men as lovers but what appealed to her about Saunière was that he was forbidden as a priest and, most importantly, he was connected with the Secret Treasure, which gave him a mystical attraction which, in Emma's eyes, more than made up for his appearance and rough nature. Added to that, when he had first made love to her she had discovered his extraordinary talent for lovemaking that may have had its roots in long repression and yearning for a woman but hit her like a thunderbolt."

"How can you possibly know that?" queried Bernard.

"Put it down to a woman's intuition and my psychic abilities," smiled Madeleine as she looked coquettishly at him.

"So if you are right we have got the Emma connection nailed!"

"Nailed? Poouff..." Madeleine gave a Parisienne pout. "Merde, what does that mean? But I have solved it! Now it's on to the Dalí connection with Rennes-le-Château...let's go tomorrow morning to the Musée Dalí in Montmartre!"

L'Espace Dalí is a small characteristically Montmartre house just behind the famous Place du Tertre, where numerous painters occupy the centre of the square, hunched over their easels producing picture postcard scenes of Paris to sell to passing tourists. This hothouse of mediocrity contrasts with the mad genius's output crammed into the small rooms in Dalí's own Montmartre space. One can't help reflect that it is not likely that any of the nearby artists will one day have an Espace to themselves in Montmartre.

Madeleine and Bernard bought their tickets from the receptionist who quickly put away her nail polish as they approached. They soon found themselves wandering almost alone among the extraordinary paintings, sculptures and jewellery on show.

Madeleine said, "C'est étonnant how Dalí has so many strange images from his dreams."

"Yes, Freud would have loved our friend Salvador, he was as familiar with his unconscious mind as he was...look, Madeleine!" Bernard had stopped by a curious elephant standing on spindly legs and with a pyramid on its back. "This is just like Bernini's elephant that I saw outside Sopra Minerva in Rome. Well, not exactly the same, as Bernini's was classical, but here is the proof that Dalí was inspired when he visited that church to create this elephant. The elephant with the pyramid is one of the links in our search."

Bernard was getting very excited and Madeleine shrieked

with amazed excitement too. "It's strange too how the tall pyramid on the elephant is echoed by the Eiffel Tower." Their talk caught the attention of a well dressed lady who was the only other visitor they had been aware of.

"Excusez moi. I could not help hearing what you said." Her English was impeccable but a tinge of accent marked the lady out as a French woman. "This elephant that intrigues you, it is important to me too. My mother was once a model for Dalí and she has talked to me about how the elephant obsessed him."

Bernard and Madeleine were wide eyed. This was synchronicity, or the fates were involved, with the appearance of this lady in this place at this time thought Bernard. Before they left the museum they conferred and decided to ask the mysterious French lady to join them for coffee. To their delight she agreed. Her name was Ernestine. They met up at La Mère Catherine an hour later, viewing the frantic hustle of the arty square from the table with the best viewing point in the Place.

Ernestine explained she had an apartment near the Parc Monceau. "They filmed Gigi there you know. I remember seeing Maurice Chevalier standing in front of the camera as they kept doing a retake of him singing 'Sank 'eaven for leettle girls.' But tell me what is your interest in Dalí and the elephant?"

They told her of their discovery of Dalí's connection with the Mystery of Rennes-le-Château.

"Ah, Rennes," she said, "you are another one of those

Dali's Elephant

treasure seekers!"

"You could say so, in a way, but we have been following a different trail from anyone else which all started with my finding a Dalí note in the church with the devil Asmodeus. It sent me a bit crazy with the whole thing and ever since I'm afraid I got Madeleine involved with me in this ridiculous search which has led us to Perpignan where Dalí called the railway station the Centre of the Universe."

"Ah oui?" shrugged Ernestine.

"...Dalí's house in Port Lligat, a Bernini statue in Rome, Titus Arch, the Garnier Opéra and now here in Montmartre where you appear to be our final piece of the jigsaw."

Ernestine was a little surprised but controlled her excitement. "Mes amis," she said, "it would be a pleasure for me if you would honour me with your company at my apartment tomorrow evening and I will see if I can help you with what you are looking for. My mother was a remarkable woman and it was she whose story may help you now. Are you free tomorrow?"

"Ah oui!"

Mme Ernestine Armand rose from the table, picked up her Dalí catalogue and umbrella and, with a charming smile, said, "à bientôt, à demain à huit heures. My card."

Madeleine and Bernard watched, still feeling slightly stunned by the encounter, as Ernestine disappeared into the tourist crowd.

After a splendid dinner of gambas, confit de canard and crème catalan accompanied by Blanquette de Limoux and

Fitou wine, Ernestine Armand looked over her spectacles, "J'adore the cuisine of Languedoc so I hope you share my enthusiasm a little."

"Absolument," whispered Madeleine as she sipped the rich red wine and remembered that first occasion with Bernard in the Auberge du Vigneron in Cucugnan. There where they had gazed up at the Cathar Château de Quéribus and drank the Fitou named after Guilhelm Bélibaste, the last Cathar.

The apartment overlooked the splendid golden gates of Parc Monceau. Madeleine was looking at the white limousine disgorging a bridal couple as they were directed into the best position for a romantic shot against the backdrop of a statue of, what looked from a distance, like Debussy.

"It's a pretty scene n'est ce pas?" Ernestine turned away from the window and gestured to the sofa. Madeleine let out a gasp of surprise as she saw she was being invited to sit on Dali's Mae West's lips sofa.

"Mon dieu c'est surréalisme!"

"I am so pleased to be able to have the opportunity to tell someone at last the story of my mother, Françoise. She was Dali's model for a few months in 1930. It was she who led him to the Mystery of Rennes-le-Château, the mystery that came to obsess him and, one could say, inspire him to create a magical game involving the Magdalene and the secret which he shared with Grand Masters of the Priory of Sion. As he followed that amazing legend, or history? He, the great surrealist and always a creative thinker. Some thought him mad but he was right when he said, 'The only difference between me and a mad man is that I am not mad.' He appreciated his fantastic and unique mind, you see, it was the source of his originality as an artist and a human being. Who else do you think could invent the idea of a railway station being the Centre of the Universe and have a statue erected to him for it. Even now you can go to Perpignan and find a sign that points to the station saying 'Le Centre de l'Univers.' Alors, my dears, I digress. You know, I think of myself in the same stream of womanhood as Gertrude Stein. I, too, am a discoverer of new creative talents. As she discovered and supported Picasso, I have found some great new artists here in Paris. I will show you their work, take you to their studios if you are here next week..." She trailed off and it was only later that they could get her back on track to tell Françoise's story.

"You may be wondering about the sofa you are sitting on?"

"Yes, we saw it at the Dalí Museum in Figueras in the Mae West Room," said Madeleine.

"Alors, this is another one of his sofas but exactly the same design and it was given to my mother by Dalí himself. She had to arrange for the transport and she hired a man with a donkey to take it over the hill from Port Lligat to Cadaques and then to Perpignan station. She had what you call a love/hate relationship with it. It was, you see, a sofa on which she had made love with the Master and she had become a bit obsessed with him but had to leave before Gala chased her out of the house.

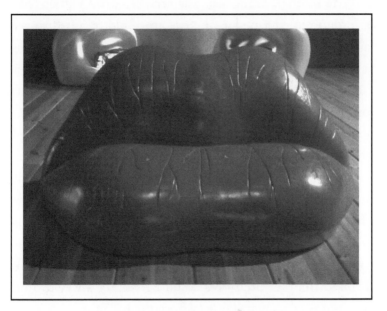

Dali's Mae West Lips Sofa

"My mother, Françoise, was very beautiful but she was also quite uneducated as she was the child of a bell ringer and a girl from a peasant family in the Languedoc. She had a wonderful childhood though. Her father was crazy about her, he never expected to be a father a second time but his pride in his daughter was très fort, very strong so his head did not rule his actions if you know what I mean? He loved the little girl but he wanted her to have more than he did. He taught her about his big secret. From when she was only four years old she knew all the details of the treasures which the Abbé Saunière had found in the town of Rennes-le-Château. This became her own personal legend so when she grew up she never forgot it. She was very pretty and soon realised that her prettiness could be for her a way to find adventure and a new life away from the backward villages of the Languedoc. She had liked drawing when a little girl and though she wasn't specially talented she liked being around artists and there were always some she could hang out with in the cafés and bars of towns like Quillan or Foix. One night she was flirting with a young man who bought her several glasses of wine and Manuel, the young man, managed that night to, so to say, enjoy her charms in his bed. Manuel was not a particularly good artist himself but was very charming... and he knew where a real genius lived.

"'He is a mad genius, this man, he is Spanish and his name is Salvador Dalí. He will become very famous. I will introduce you, no better, I will recommend you to him as his model. When he sees you he will be ecstatic, but beware he may not paint you as you really are, as he will turn you into some strange creation of his mind.'...Françoise went to Port Lligat to meet Dalí and this meeting was her crossroads and, for Dalí, the magic moment when he met the mystery of Rennes-le-Château!"

Bernard and Madeleine smiled at each other. They had been led, mysteriously enough, to the one person who could put the last piece in the puzzle.

That night the mystery ended. Dalí's extraordinary journey had been unravelled by Bernard and Madeleine.

Chapter 16

London 2005

The French church in London is just off Leicester Square. Thronging outside the Empire were restless crowds awaiting the arrival of Judi Dench for the premiere of Mrs Henderson, the story of the Windmill Theatre. Bernard squeezed past excited fans and girls waving other kinds of fans in front of them as they smiled at the cameras in their role as the Windmill girls. "We never closed," thought Bernard as he hurried on, hoping that was true of the Catholic church too.

Inside the church the energy was as calm as it was frantic outside. It didn't take long to find it, Jean Cocteau's masterpiece, the fresco of the Crucifixion, which he painted in 1943 at the behest of the Priory of Sion. The secret is hidden but not to those who know, he thought. And there it was. The magical rose at the foot of the cross, an apparent decorative device or much more? The rose as a symbol for Mary Magdalene and regeneration of the Sacred Feminine.

He sighed thinking of Madeleine and the roses he had had delivered to her at her apartment in the 16th in Paris. His note had said "Madeleine, merci for the journey. From your man of mystery." He knew she would know the meaning of the roses.

His mobile rang (damn, he had forgotten to turn it off).

"Bonjour chéri," a woman's voice said, "merci Bernard pour les roses."

"I'm in church!" he whispered.

"Non, not again!"

"Listen Madeleine, I've found Cocteau's rose and I think I've found a hidden message. It's..."

"Stop, arrete! These roses, there is a hidden message here? And I think it says will you not come to London? Is that not properly decoded?" she purred.

"Yes, yes, follow the clues and you'll get to the Gare du Nord and then Waterloo."

"Bernard, will you be there or will you be locked in church again?"

Bernard had gone to France to escape his feelings over his failed marriage and now, what he had thought was a holiday romance had turned over his world. Had he found his personal Holy Grail or was he an incarnation of a troubadour admiring his chosen woman as the embodiment of the Sacred Feminine? Whatever the meaning he knew he wanted to welcome Madeleine to London.

"I'll be there chérie. You are the only mystery I want to explore now. A bientôt!"

Jean Cocteau's fresco of the Crucifixion